Come, Time

Richard Jenkins

CHAPTER ONE

Why does God need people? What use are we to Him? In His possession is absolute knowledge, so what can God learn from people? Why create people? What's the point of doing anything when you know it all already? He knows the beginning, and the end of each and every one of us, but still we keep coming, faster and faster, spamming His world with nothing He doesn't already know, with nothing He hasn't already seen. We enter His world and face two exits. We are tested, judged. We dare to live and fear to die. We can pass into heaven or fail into Hell. You created me God, but you knew I would ultimately fail. Was I necessary? Was I needed? Did you need me, God? Or am I weight, just ballast? A spec of junkie dust? What can you gain watching me suffer here or forever in Hell?

Does this, us, make Him happy or sad? Can we move God to tears? Can we make him smile? If we fail to educate Him, is our purpose to entertain? Is life an audition for God? Well if so, look away, God, look away from me. I seek no recognition. I need no fame.

God, in my mind, is insane. Imagine knowing everything; imagine needing to do nothing and having eternity to do it in. Imagine having no hunger, no need or urge to know. Nothing would ever surprise you. Nothing would ever challenge you. You would exist in a singular state. Nothing would ever change, not even time. Nothing would really exist.

Why bother with people? Does He consume our souls? Do people have value? Is God addicted to beauty, to perfection, in finding it in something other than Him?

All this drama, it all seems a bit much to me, but then I am a simple man. My use to God, I dig graves. I earn money from death. In the countryside, you can often earn a few quid digging a home for the dead. I enjoy it. It's one of my most favorite jobs, even in a winter freeze when the earth becomes one, a solid, zipped-up mass. I'm good at it, too. Not a boast you'll often hear, but digging a grave satisfies well. Nothing morbid, you'll understand. To me, it's thirty quid cash-in-hand and a full body workout. Hard, manual labour can get me high.

Anyway, grave dug, job done. The final resting place of Tony Spence, who died from a heart attack aged just fifty-two, born 1952 died this year 2011, a local man who I'd acknowledge with a smile or a nod of the head, whose death has inspired great pity and sadness and created the catch phrase,

1

'Just fifty-two, so young, too young to die.'

But then tell that to the billions who came before him. To all but a few the life of Tony Spence would seem divine. He was never short of food; he was never out of work. Not once did he fear for his life; not once was he told to kill. His house was solid and rightfully his own. He travelled to foreign lands as a free man, for pleasures as simple as lying in the sun. All his children lived. At forty-five, when a mole on his shoulder became cancerous, a medicine man cured him, not with magic but with science. Of course, as modern wisdom insists, his fondness for cigarettes, pastries and beer pushed him hard to an early grave. But did he care? Should we? Historically speaking, he lived a long and successful life. In the history of humankind, Tony Spence was a winner.

My time is up, my thirty minutes gone. I'm lying in the grave looking up at a near cloudless sky - my usual practice once I've finished digging a grave. I enter the earth to rest and think. To let my thoughts drift with the clouds. Not that they ever do. They always seem stuck on a topic that is rarely of my choosing. Often, I hear people, those visiting the dead, their feet on gravel, rarely the spoken word, but only once, and then a child, has someone looked down into the freshly dug grave to witness me resting. The child, a boy of about eight, on seeing me asked,

'What are you doing down there?' I should have replied,

'Keeping it warm.' But I didn't. I smiled, shrugged and stared.

I live off the land. I hunt, forage, grow and poach. When you live by the coast, you can always find food. I eat well, better than most: fresh fish and seafood that I catch myself; fresh game, poached of course by me. I even rustle the occasional sheep, and the farmer's crop I treat as my own.

I live isolated, perched on a cliff top, in a four birth caravan on an acre of land, which I bought for a single week's labour. Cheap, you may think, but listen, hear the sea work the cliff, hear it smash and grab the earth and rock. In three years time, my land will be gone, erased and fully consumed, a tenant of the sea once more.

The area where I live has never been a tourist haven. The coastline is too wild, the beaches too pebbled. Only walkers seem to visit. Today, however, we have marked the map, and the map has called us treasure town.

It is a brisk, autumn afternoon. Thick, sunken cloud docks in the sky above. Embraced by a beautiful wind, I walk along a ragged stretch of coastline on my way to gather mussels. This should be a solitary affair but today I am joined by people, crazed, manic people. Some are local, most are not. Whole families are out to snatch the bounty.

The full details, to me, are vague, but we have made the news, captured the public's imagination. A cargo ship, which failed to hug a storm, has spilled forty or so containers. The contents of which, from toys to homewares, unable to resist the desire of the people, have been pulled towards this beach, and now the people embrace the bounty as if a suddenly found long lost relative, a rich one at that.

Two women mother and daughter would be my guess, bred in the fashion of Chinese Whispers, both wearing near identical sportswear and both carrying that fat gene, the one activated after eating copious amounts of cake, furiously drag a reluctant bounty laden shopping trolley up along the beach. I know that modern women, men too, like to own things, but thirty sets of cutlery? Thank God no one invites me to weddings. The beach becomes steep, the pebbles sharp and slippery. The trolley becomes stuck; their fury thickens. The trolley is now the latest scum that clogs their passage through life that conspires to deny them all that is rightfully theirs. They stop, unable to progress. One pulls out a mobile phone and makes a call. Somewhere a skinny man with emotional problems splutters into life. Seagulls glide on the wind looking down, picking up tips.

I scramble up a grassy embankment onto a narrow footpath. Instantly my scent is snatched by a TV News film crew, one of six out hustling for the action. Without hesitation, the Anchorwoman charges towards me, her microphone thrust forward and aimed directly at my face. A crew of two dutifully follows. Her smile glitters through the grey of the day. She rapidly nears me. I hear her purr,

'Are you local? Can I ask you some questions? We are the news!'

They are the news. I thought we were the news. I have no intention of stopping. I lower my head and stare at the ground, enough body language to inform them all of my intent. The purr begins to growl.

'We're national! This is your chance to be on national television!'

They block the path. I continue to walk. The Anchorwoman stops; I do not. Her reactions are good. She just manages to twist her body beyond my course. The cameraman fails to react so gets lightly shouldered aside, as does the soundman.

'Oh for fuck's sake,' she snaps, with bemused contempt.

I turn to look at the news. The Anchorwoman stares at me with a look of absolute contempt. A look I know well.

'Bashful, are we? Grow some fuckin' balls!' she continues.

Heard that said, too, only said with more aggression.

What is it with balls? Everyone wants balls, especially people in suits. Get balls, be ruthless. Fine by me, but why draw the line? What if I now pulled out a knife and took it to her throat? What if I answered her with a cold, ruthless action? Would she congratulate me for having king-sized, made-of-steel balls?

My father, who was a violent man, loved to recall how he and an army friend once beat the living daylights out of four Punk Rockers. The irony, of course, which my father knew, was that the Punks, who claimed to be anarchists, ran to the arms of the fascist police for safety and to demand the arrest my father and his friend. As my father would say, they got taught a proper life lesson and all for fuckin' free.

I wouldn't volunteer to live in a society without laws, but if it happened, then I believe I would prosper, certainly I would survive. Would the mid-ranking men and women in suits? I leave the knife in my pocket and politely flash them a smile.

I gather the mussels quickly. The tide is starting to turn and will soon rapidly rise. The mussels grow on a six decayed wooden jetties that have long stopped having any other use. In the distance, to my left, I can see the scavengers, all high on their own good fortune, and all blissfully unaware of how quickly the tide will turn. To my right, set back against a foaming sky, a Land Rover ambles slowly away. It is the same Land Rover that I have already encountered four times in the last two days. Now, I'm not classifying this as suspicious, but five times, in my isolated world and each time in a separate location? Whoever sits in that Land Rover may not be watching me, but me, now, I am watching them.

CHAPTER TWO

My day had nearly finished. The time is 9.38 p.m. I am at home in my caravan, well fed and warm. I am standing at a window, peering through the curtain, watching a car as it pulls up outside. I am expecting no visitors, I never do. The car engine is switched off, the headlights follow. The shape of a Land Rover silhouetted against a moon-lit sky is revealed. I step away, stand still and wait.

Two cars doors open then gently close. I hear no voices. Footsteps approach. A short, sharp, not too loud knock on the door. I wait, let them knock again. Seven seconds later they do. The knock is exactly the same - no increased force considered necessary. I open the door, and in the murk of the night, see two men and a Police wallet-badge raised for me to read.

'Mr. Dean, we're Police. We need to speak to you. Don't worry; we're aware of your disability.'

I have a disability? I assume they mean that I am a mute. They both seem serious and, unless armed, physically not a threat. Both are touching forty and dressed as company men in smart, office clothing. Both are lean, fit and seemingly healthy. The badge I ignore, it tells me nothing. I mean, how can I tell if it's real? I gesture for them to enter, which they calmly do.

'My name is Phillip; this is my colleague, Andrew.'

First name terms already. No constable or detective. Phillip continues,

'We're from Special Branch.'

I stare at them passively, remaining outwardly calm. Inside a swirl of confusion, is this serious or ridiculous? When spoken, it sounds both. They stare back at me, solid and without reaction. Should I believe them? I could ask them to prove it but what good would that do? They couldn't. All I can do is let them speak; let them say what they've come to say.

We crowd around a small dining table. We are bunched tightly together, but neither of them seems uncomfortable. There is a fresh pot of coffee sitting on the stove; its smell is loud and delicious. I offer them nothing, but neither seems to care. Andrew pulls out a notepad and pen from his coat pocket then slides them towards me. Phillip places the black leather folder he has been holding down on the table then quickly gets down to business.

'Mr. Dean,' he says, 'firstly let me make it clear, you are not in any trouble. We are not investigating you or anyone you personally know. Our visit is for one reason and one reason only and, that is to ask for your help.'

5

He opens up the folder. I see a photo of a house that looks familiar. He slides the photo towards me and continues to explain.

'This property, it's familiar to you,' he continues.

It is, so I nod my head.

'It's isolated, but you pass it on a regular basis when you're out poaching or foraging for food.'

Again, the truth, so I nod.

'Recently the property has been bought by this woman.'

From the folder, he hands me a second photograph. It is of a woman standing outside the house. She is about sixty years of age, a pensioner hippy-chick dressed in colourful woolens, the sort you can buy at craft fairs. Somehow I think she looks wise, with skin regularly refreshed by the great outdoors. She is smiling even though she seems to be alone. Phillip continues,

'Now, what we can tell you about this woman, and we can tell you this with absolute certainly, is that this woman plays an active role within the animal liberation movement.'

Without pause the double act begins; Andrew breaks his silence.

'She's a key player.'

'A figurehead,' adds Phillip.

'Not as physically active as she once was, but as an organizer, as an inspirer, she is still very much an important figure.'

Silence. They both look at me for a reaction, but I give them nothing. Andrew continues, somewhat impatiently.

'Her views are extreme. Do we need to explain them to you?'

I shake my head. He continues.

'Do you sympathise with her views? Do you have any sympathy at all for what she believes in?'

Phillip rolls in seamlessly.

'If you do, you must tell us, you must tell us now.'

I shake my head.

'You're saying no?'

I nod.

'Good. As we thought.'

They pause, watching me, making sure. Convinced, Andrew continues, his impatience settled.

'We want you to watch the house. We need you to tell us when either of these two men visit, which in time they will.'

Andrew fans out eight photos on the table, all are ten by eight inches in size. They show candid surveillance shots of two average looking men, both aged around thirty. In none of the photos are the two men seen together.

'These are dangerous men,' says Andrew.

In your opinion.

'Not one-on-one,' adds Phillip.

'They're terrorists. Cowards. They harm from a far. The sort of men it's easy to hate.'

Pull me in. Let us hate together. Phillip continues.

'We can't talk specifics, but we need to know when they visit her.'

'This doesn't mean we want you to set up a surveillance unit on a twenty four seven basis. We're simply asking you to be aware, to be vigilant. To pass the property in the morning and at night. To follow your usual routine, nothing more.'

'To react to any intelligence that we feed you.'

'When they show up, which they will, for a period of two to three days, all you need to do is make contact with us.'

'Make a note of any car number plates and any other details you think important. If anyone else visits, then do the same.'

'Simple but important.'

There is a pause. Being a mute, pauses don't unsettle me like they do other people. I can quite happily stare someone silently in the eye without a care in the world. Andrew sees this and breaks the silence.

'Why you? Why are we asking you? Well, there's the obvious reason you're local, you know the area, it wouldn't be unusual for you to be seen in the area or to be seen carrying binoculars or wearing camouflage.'

'Of course, we know other locals who fit the bill but none of them are quite like you, are they, Mr. Dean?'

I offer no response. Unfazed he continues.

'It's also a question of resources. We have none.'

He smiles. He wants me to share his truthful joke. We're all mates now. I return no smile. Phillip brings the matter back to business.

'Or rather, what we do have quickly runs out. The service is under a lot of pressure. I'm sure you can understand that, and that animal liberation is not exactly our priority.'

I can. It's hardly the glamour gig in this day and age.

'To be perfectly honest, you're the easiest option.'

'So, can we count on you?'

I write on the notepad, 'I don't work for nothing.' Seeing my words Andrew is quick to reply.

'A payment, of course, if reasonable.'

I add to the note 'A thousand pounds, cash.' Again his reply is instant.

'Done. So we have a deal, Mr. Dean?'

I nod and agree to take my second job of the day. Jesus, call me a rat I must be joining the race. They both look ever so slightly relieved and pleased with themselves. Phillip glances at Andrew then speaks.

'Well, that was all very, civilised.'

They share a smile then focus on me.

'Do you have mobile phone?' Andrew asks.

I shake my head.

'I assume you know how to use one?'

I nod. From his inside jacket pocket, he pulls out a mobile phone and charger then places them on the table.

'For you. Standard, simple to use. In the contacts is one number, our number. If you need to contact us, use it, text us. Oh, and business only. Over step the mark with personal calls and you'll have the most feared men in the service after you, the accountants.'

They both laugh. I force a slight smile.

'That's not a joke. They will check the bill. Anyway, to reiterate, if either of these two men visits, which they will in the next month or so, then we need to know A.S.A.P. That is your prime objective. If they arrive in a vehicle, then take the details. If anyone else visits, then do the same. That's all we require of you. Is that clear?'

I nod. He continues.

'These people assume they are under surveillance. It's not in your interest, or ours, for you to take any unnecessary risks. Neither is it in your interest, or ours, for you to tell anyone what we have asked you to do, or in fact to tell anyone anything we have said here tonight. Is that understood?'

I write, 'It is. Now, what about the cash?'

After fetching the money from the Land Rover, they leave.

I sit at the dining table and study my bounty: a thousand pounds in twenty pound notes, a mobile phone and charger, a notepad and pen and eight photos of two men wanted by Special Branch. Not a bad haul, but then life never deals straightforward, unambiguous positives and tonight is no exception.

One of the photos concerns me. It shows one of the men, his back to the camera, his head turned to look behind. He is wearing a t-shirt tucked into a pair of jeans. The jeans are Levi's 501 Red Tab. The waistband Red Tab label is clearly visible, as is the red Levi material tag that is stitched to the left side of the right back pocket. My concern is simple; the Red Tab label is made from suede. Now, wouldn't a man involved in the animal liberation movement, involved to terrorist level, be a vegan? Wouldn't he be savvy enough to know a label on his jeans was an animal product and so point blank against all that he believes in? To my mind, he would. So why is he wearing the jeans? Maybe he's undercover, posing as someone who couldn't give a shit, but that would be stupid. A man who assumes he is being watched by the government undercover for his cause? Maybe he's a double agent. Maybe this man was himself an agent of Special Branch and the photo shows him in Civvy Street. Maybe this man has nothing to do with the animal liberation movement and is instead wanted for something completely different.

I have been in the employ of Special Branch for less than fifteen minutes, and already I am becoming paranoid.

My day had nearly finished. All was calm and settled. My only pressing decision was one whisky or three. I could have said no. If all had seemed well and genuine, I would have, but it didn't so I said, yes. I couldn't resist. I will not walk away from a lie.

Could someone be trying to mess with me, playing a practical joke? But then who would play it? No one I know, after all I know so few and those I do, would have more sense. Maybe I am over reacting. Maybe there is a true and valid reason why he's wearing the jeans. After all, even people with serious, passionate causes can be stupid. The majority of people I've met who have held deep, unmovable beliefs have seemed pretty thick to me. If the human race has one true genius, it's the ability to adapt, to think freely and to understand, at some level at least, that there is no one, singular, absolute truth. Many a stupid man has been empowered by an ideology. It saves them from having to think for themselves and provides easy, ready-made quotes and answers. It wraps them up all snug and warm in the collective acceptance of others.

Of course, this man may be a psychopath, and animal liberation an easy route to violence, murder and pain. I mean, how many psychopaths have used a political cause to satisfy their psycho desires? Two percent of the population is thought to be psychopathic. Now violence is always in the hands of the minority, but what minority, two percent? What percentage of Catholic men in Northern Ireland joined the IRA to kill and maim?

Animal liberation, my honest opinion, depends on my mood, depends on the image. See a monkey chained, his eyes silently screaming why, then gladly I'll sign the petition, but such an image will quickly fade as I get back to my own survival.

The most interesting animal experiment I know of is this: two mice kept in large, separate cages. Both cages were full of twisting tunnels, and natural vegetation. One mouse was given all the food he could eat, and guess what, he got fat and lazy. When he wasn't sleeping, he was sitting perfectly still, waiting for the time he could feast again. The other mouse was given hardly any food, certainly not enough to survive, and guess what, he stayed sharp and active, lean and healthy. He spent his day scurrying around the cage investigating, looking for food. He was happier, healthier and lived longer.

So if you can stay hungry whilst all around are feasting....

I could contact them, text them on the phone and demand an explanation, but why should I? I'm sure they could come up with a plausible explanation. What good would it do me? The only thing to do is to play along, to act out what I have agreed to do.

CHAPTER THREE

The cottage does indeed stand isolated and alone but as a place to hide from prying eyes, it is useless. It is perfectly exposed, no trees, hedges or fence attempt to obscure it from view. The landscape that surrounds it is hilly pasture and woodland. As a defensive position, it is futile. I could hide in the woodland. They would never see me.

The cottage was until recently up for sale. I remember seeing the "For Sale" and "Sold" signs. It can't have been cheap, either. My guess, three hundred grand at least, and that's now, 2010, in recession. Four bedrooms, full of character, in good repair and with half an acre of land. One old lady living alone, but surviving on more than a state pension. The half acre of land is unkempt and without any specific purpose, no flowers, vegetables or well kept lawn make use of it, which is exactly how the previous owner left it. Parked outside the cottage is a 2006 Nissan Micra. For now, I will assume this is the woman's car.

It is 6.30 a.m. and not yet fully light. I am hiding in a patch of woodland. Using my binoculars, I observe the front of the cottage. Through the kitchen window, I can see the woman. She is wearing a blue dressing gown and is standing perfectly still as if listening to something intently. On a kitchen table, I can see a radio. Suddenly, she becomes animated, her body language dismissive. A wave of contempt pulses across her face, and she seems to mouth the words, 'Oh, fuck off!' Shaking her head, she turns and quickly paces away.

Through a second downstairs window, I see her enter a room. She hurries to a desk, sits and begins to work on a laptop computer. I cannot see the screen.

She continues working, typing furiously away for an hour and twenty minutes. During this time I scan what I can and, although my view is limited, I see no obvious signs of protest. Nothing makes me suspicious. I'm sure this woman has passions, and maybe even causes to fight for, but am I really watching the hub of radical animal liberation? Maybe I am, but to be sure, I need to get closer.

For the rest of the day I shop. They paid me a grand, and regardless of how I, the woman, Special Branch play out, I'm keeping it. I stock up on food, on basic supplies. I then treat myself. I buy a new coat, not one to appease the latest fashion, but one to take on the elements, likewise a pair of boots. I then go to the butchers and buy a rib of beef, a family joint for six. An expensive cut of meat, but one I will consume in a single, joyful sitting. The rest of the money will be hidden, stashed away for a moment unknown.

It is 4.05 p.m. I am hurrying down a country lane on my way to watch the cottage. The night is quickly approaching and will soon smother what remains of the day. In the distance, I can hear a car lumbering towards me.

The lane is narrow and twisting, edged with tall hedges that act as blinkers. Hearing the car reach the corner ahead I step off the road and onto a narrow grass verge, where I stand waiting for the car to pass - an act of self-preservation. The sound of a car slowly approaching is no guarantee of one competently driven. The car cautiously appears from around the corner. It is the Nissan Micra parked outside the cottage. Inside, I see the Woman, driving. Seeing me, she brakes and slows to a pace that is polite but which is also unnecessary slow. As the car rolls towards me, she looks at me and smiles. I reply with a nod and a smile; both feel somewhat awkward. Her stare and smile continue. Time slows. Finally, the car reaches me, as it passes she manages to keep her smile fixed on me for a few seconds more by turning to look out of the driver's side window. Her smile widens, and her eyes seem to say 'There, we made it.' As she accelerates away, she toots her horn twice.

We have made first contact; we have looked each other in the eye, and without saying a word I told her a lie. In my world, she is significant, a fact that is known to me. In her world, I am significant, a fact that is unknown to her. How many such shadows follow us around?

Now, unless she is on her way to visit someone who lives close-by, and there aren't many people who live close-by, the nearest, rational, location for her to visit, a local village shop, is twenty minutes away minimum. This gives me forty minutes to move in closer, forty minutes to put the lie to rest.

Five minutes later, I reach the cottage. I scan the view; nothing alerts me to the presence of people. Darkness is fifteen minutes away. I could play it safe and wait, or I could make my move now. Given the odds that hidden eyes are watching me my decision is easy. I approach the cottage. The hall light is on. I walk directly to the front door and knock loudly. Silence. I knock again. Silence. I try the door; it's locked. I turn to face behind, take several paces away then turn back and hurry towards the rear of the cottage. Here I see two doors. I try to open the first. It is bolted shut, but the give is considerable. An an inside bolt fixed to the top of the door is all that holds it firm. I concentrate my force over the bolt, and the door opens.

I step inside and close the door. Inspecting the bolt for damage, I see none. The catch on the door frame is loose, but no wood has splintered away. I turn a few screws and conceal my entry.

The house smells of baking. I am standing in the kitchen, and the welcoming smell of fresh pastry hangs sweetly in the air. I take several deep breathes, and my pounding heart begins to ease. My gran, who for a time brought me up, could always soothe my moods with an afternoon of her magic baking.

The light is low, but I have no trouble locating the fridge. I move to it and open the door, inside: bacon, cheese, eggs and milk, an organic salmon fillet, salami and a pork chop. We all have guilty pleasures, but can this really be the fridge of an animal liberation extremist? To my mind no, it cannot.

I decide to leave. I know I could stay and dig deeper; rummage through her belongings and look for clues, but what right do I have? I have trespassed long enough. This woman has only ever smiled at me. She wasn't the one who told me a lie.

Passing a kitchen table I find a laptop. The screen is on; I can't resist a look. It shows a web page, address https://boxxx5481422.com/oakley. A casual scan of the text heavy page suggests an academic report on the subject of growing algae. Is she an academic? She has the look. Next to the laptop is an empty bottle of wine. Has she gone for supplies?

I exit through the second back door and head back to the caravan for whiskey, beef, and thought.

I am alone in the caravan sitting in silence for tonight the elements are still. The beef was delicious and the whiskey a warm embrace. I should feel contented; however, loose-ends nag me. I don't like it when people complicate things. My life is simple, it's what I have chosen. Some people get off on drama and constant complications I, however, do not. I like routine. Change is fine when it's paced with the seasons, but, ultimately, with a routine I can trust myself, with a routine I can know myself.

I decide to do nothing, to pull myself out of the loop, to continue as I was before the visit. They asked me to watch an animal rights extremist, but this was a lie, so now the contract has been broken, and the deal is off. For all I care, Phillip and Andrew can come and go along with the truth of the situation. I care for neither. It would be easy to sit here a slave to my imagination, a slave to the question, why, but I don't desire to know the truth. I desire my own peace of mind. If, in time, I am confronted by the truth then fine; I am more than willing to defend myself, but for now, for me, the adventure has finished.

So quiet is the sea I step outside to check it still exists. It does, as does the wind. I will sleep outside tonight, and tomorrow I will continue as I normally would.

CHAPTER FOUR

It has been said numerous times that a criminal will often return to the scene of their crime. This is something I have always thought stupid; however, the next day I do not resist the urge of walking past the cottage. Admittedly, I am on my way to do other business, but still, I stop and stare. The Nissan Micra is once again parked outside, but I see no other sign of the woman at home. The hall light remains on; no curtains are drawn, and all other house lights are switched off.

I quickly move on. The best time to shoot rabbits is early morning and today, this is my only goal.

Early evening, and again I pass the cottage. All remains the same: the car, the lights, the curtains. It would be easy to assume the woman is out.

The following day, I fight the urge to go to the cottage. By nightfall, I am standing in woodland looking down on a scene that refuses to change. The car, the hall light, the curtains are all as before, and all other house lights remain off.

All is probably fair and rational. I have suspicions but only ones that concern a pensioner living alone - a trip or a fall in a house that smothers your scream. I could find her in need, but if I did, how would I justify my presence? Through lies or confession? I cannot find her by accident. She could simply be out, she probably is. I'm speculating, procrastinating. I cut myself off and decide to move.

I hurry to the cottage, straight to the front door which I knock loudly. No one answers. I knock again. No one answers. I rush away to the first back door. I apply the correct force to the correct location and push the door open.

I step inside, stand perfectly still and strain to hear any sound. Silence. No sound of human occupation. The smell of baking has gone, replaced by the smell of rotting household waste, both vegetable and flesh. I stand in darkness. The only artificial light is that from the hall, which spills through the gaps of an ill fitting door. I move to this door and open it. My eyes take the first wave of light with a beat of pain and a heavy blink. Quickly, however, I see and what is it I see? I see her, the woman, in the hall, slumped on the floor, her head and face bludgeoned. I freeze, speechless of course, but also thoughtless. For a time, I do not know how long, I stick to this moment, this snap of time, and then, I wake. I do not panic. I do not fear. I feel no revulsion, disgust or even anger. All I feel is sadness, sadness for this woman. I kneel beside her and hold her hand and of course it is cold and stiff but still it feels human. My gaze turns in on itself, and I see her face from memory - her smiling, pleasant face. But then, suddenly, I wake once more. I drop her hand as my thoughts start shouting, what are the consequences, the consequences for me?

Now sickness turns in my gut. Now my stare is drawn to her face. Now I see the horror of what truly is before me. I see the present and flashes of the past, this woman hit once then battered beyond death. Murdered for business and pleasure. I see the horror in her stare as she takes the blows. I see her staring at me, directly at me, but I wasn't there! She and others are staring at me, but I wasn't there! I am not the witness to her last, final scream.

Instinct propels me to leave, but I resist and force myself to stay. I cannot run away. Something cold and ruthless has caused this, and now, if I am to face it, I too must find a chill in my soul. I stand trying to think clearly, trying to resist the call of flight. I am in her house; I've broken in, and my fingerprints wait to snare me. Using the sleeve of my coat, I vigorously wipe the interior door handle, then the fridge door, then all other areas corrupted by my touch. My coat, my new coat, bought with their money. Good. For tomorrow, I will burn it, along with everything else I am wearing.

Will my fingerprints be on her hand? I refuse the risk and wipe it anyway. Her fingers are long and slender, her nails without varnish. I look for rings; there are none, no watch or bracelets. I look at her crushed and broken face then down at her neck, where I see no necklace. Her blood-matted hair covers her ears. I hesitate for a second, then brush the hair away. I notice her pierced left ear holds no earring.

I stand and see my muddy footprints covering the tiled hall floor. I need a mop. I find the kitchen light switch and with my sleeve covered hand turn it on. Instantly my reflection in the kitchen window pounces. I feel watched, observed in the distance. I rush to the window and kill my reflection with the pull of a blind.

Muddied footprints cover the kitchen floor. I kick off my boots and then cover my hand with a tea towel. I look for a mob and quickly find one, bucket and all. Frantically, I begin to clean the floor. Evidence washes away, but do I save more than myself?

Job done. I return the mop and stuff the tea towel in my coat pocket. I pause and catch my breath.

Why murder? I quickly move through the house lightly looking for clues. Nothing is disturbed. No draws pulled out, no looting. If robbery was the motive, then the thief came with knowledge.

The urge to flight floods through my veins. I have to leave. Never have

I felt so wrong. I pause and think. Do I leave here for good? Do I take with me all traces of my visits? I think about burning the house down, a thought I barely resist, but instead I pick up my boots and move to make my exit.

Outside in the darkness, I struggle to put my boots on. Standing on one leg is impossible. All balance is void, my equilibrium is smashed.

Back at the caravan, in an oil barrel blaze all that I was wearing is destroyed.

Freshly washed, scrubbed hard, I sit naked and alone. Rarely do I feel alone, but tonight, I recognize that this is what I am, completely alone. I console myself by reminding myself that at least I am alive. I live. All that I want, which isn't much, is still within my grasp. I am more than willing to fight for it, and now, whatever comes my way.

I could call the police and submit my truth. I was watching the woman, yes, a request from two men claiming to be from Special Branch. They said it concerned animal liberation, but this I know was a lie. Do I sound convincing? No. Do I sound like a nut? Yes. And maybe that's the point, to sound like the local nut, the weirdo amongst you. He who never speaks, who lives alone, removed from normality. The hunter, the poacher. Paranoid. Dressed in camouflage, waiting for the world to end. Put me under the microscope and they've got their disease.

I was lied to. They came to my caravan and lied to me. They involved me in this, but what exactly is this? Murder, obviously, but who am I?

CHAPTER FIVE

The following day, dawn has yet to fully wake. I am once again hidden in woodland looking down on a scene that refuses to change. I take the mobile phone and write a text message,

'The two men have landed, together. Both at the cottage now.'

I select the number stored on the phone then send the message away.

Now, I wait. For what, I don't know. For helicopters to swoop in? For time to pass into nothing?

The phone beeps. I look at the screen and see the message, 'Message not sent. Message sending failed.'

I try again. The same message is returned. I check the signal strength - four bars. I call the number and hear an automated voice tell me,

'The number you have called is not recognized.'

Two lies down and increasingly, I am the fool. Maybe the mobile is faulty. I hurry away, desperate to reach the nearest phone box.

Inside the local shop. I have to buy a newspaper, to break a twenty for change. Familiar faces greet me with a smile. Am I different, tainted? Will they see my odd behavior when asked to remember?

Sheltered inside the phone box - at one with it, as lonely and redundant it stands today. I dial the number. An automated voice tells me,

'The number you have dialed has not been recognized.'

Again. One more time.

'The number you have dialed has not been recognized.'

I hurry back towards my caravan. Avoiding the roads, I go cross-country. I now expect the worst. I expect the police to find both the body and a trail, a trail which leads dishonestly to me.

I try and stay calm. I can feel anger, almost a panic, a scream to release. I must focus on the now, anchor myself to the present. I must keep control, consider what I know.

Two men call on me. They tell me they are from Special Branch and ask me to watch a woman, to look out for two men who will visit her. They claim the crime is animal liberation, all the way to terrorist level. I sense a lie and accept the challenge. I watch the woman and discover she has nothing to do with animal liberation. Two days later I find her dead, murdered brutally. The phone number they gave me doesn't work. By entering her house, I have incriminated myself. Was this their plan? How could they be sure I would? They couldn't. If I am the stooge, then there must be more, unknown plants and plots. They gave me a grand, some of which was publicly seen. Does the money call theft? Does it add up and lead to murder?

In the distance, I catch sight of the sea. The tide is crashing in. Do I ride the wave? Will I tame it? Do I swim ahead of it or has it already washed over me and left me choking, gasping for air?

I must ask no questions, myself no questions. Why me, I banish. Back to my caravan, pack what I need then vanish.

Why would anyone kill the woman? The woman, I don't even know her name. I must return to her house, risk one more visit, but this time I must look properly for clues. I am tempted to wait until nightfall before making my entry, but I cannot be still. Once packed and ready to flee I rush to the house and enter by my usual route. Standing by the backdoor, I pull off my muddy boots and ready my senses to block out any sight or smell of the woman. I am here to know her past not her present. I quickly move through the kitchen ignoring the many draws and cupboards. My first priority is her laptop, which no longer sits on the kitchen table. I enter the hall and pass the woman, who I barely acknowledge, into the study and straight to the desk. Here I find the laptop. I snatch it, leads snap out. I grab the power cable, yank it from the wall socket, wrap it around the laptop then stuff them into my rucksack. Suddenly, my focus spins to a sound outside. I look to the window and recognize the sound as a car engine. I drop to my knees. I was in full view of the window. The sound continues, getting louder, getting closer. It stops. I crawl to the side of the window, pause and listen. I hear a car door pushed shut, quickly followed by another. I raise myself up and peer out through the side of the curtain. Two suited, middle-aged men take the final few steps towards the front door. They look like police, CID. I lower myself and take cover. I strain to listen, desperate to hear any snippet of conversation, but all I can hear is my breath being pumped hard through my mouth. If they look through the letterbox, they will see the woman. I could move her. I hesitate. A loud three second knock on the door. I could move her. Another knock, louder, shorter, quickly followed by the snap of metal on metal.

In a flash I raise myself up, take a peek then lower myself into cover. One of the men was rushing towards a parked silver saloon car, his colleague, tried to shoulder the front door open. The door holds; it is heavy and solid. I slip my rucksack on then sneak another look. The man at the car reaches in through an opened front side window and grabs an in-car radio. His colleague rushes away, I assume towards the back of the house, to the first, unlocked door.

I scramble away crawling under the window. Once clear, I rise up and sprint through the hall into the kitchen. A dash to my boots. I grab them, but now where? I see a door. The backdoor shakes. I pull open the door, step inside and pull the door shut. Blackout, the darkness is complete. I am squashed into a pantry; the smell of spices mixed with marzipan and icing sugar fill the air. This is not the time for memories of youth, but I have hidden in such a pantry before. No sight, only sound. I hear the backdoor flung open then footsteps rush across the kitchen floor. Silence. Slowly and gently I begin to put on my boots. Footsteps again, rush across the kitchen floor. Then voices.

'Jesus!'

'For fuck sake!'

'Do nuisance calls lead to this?'

'God knows.'

'How long?'

'Fifteen minutes.'

Nuisance calls? Is that why they came? Wasn't she reported missing? Fifteen minutes, for back-up? I have one option, to run. Boots on, hood up, sneak out and flee. Quickly with the boots. Surely all attention is on the woman. If they see me, so what? I run, what changes? Two middle-aged men cannot catch me. The voices flare up.

'There's a message.'

I hear four electronic beeps. I think of a phone.

'What?'

'It's a mobile number.'

'What?'

'Nothing…Silence.'

'As she said…Return the call'

'Now? Should we?'

'Why not?'

Another single beep. I finish with the boots. Then suddenly, startled, I jump as a shiver vibrates through me. The mobile phone, their mobile phone, in my trouser pocket fizzes into life. It vibrates then squeals with ever increasing volume. No time to think. I shoulder the door open and spill out into the kitchen. The two police officers stand staring at me, rooted in stillness through shock. I, too, freeze. As sense returns the officer holding the phone presses a button and cancels the call. The mobile in my pocket squeals no more. I turn to run. This movement fires the officers into action. They rush towards me. I stop, then turn and attack. Four quick, hard, even brutal punches later and my pursuers writhe slowly on the floor. I need a head start. I am but one, they will be many.

I sprint out through the door. Once again I have nowhere to go but never have I ran so fast to get there. Reaching the front of the cottage I see the police car and skid to a stop. I pause, hesitating. I ask myself, 'dare I?' Instinct pleas with me to flee but still I stand, staring at the car as a voice in my head begins to scream, 'in order to survive you must take risks!'

If I run into the countryside what chance have I got? How far can I get before man, dog and machine start to hunt me down? I cannot be predictable. I must fight myself as much as I must fight everyone else.

I rush to the car and gently open the boot. A glance back reveals I still have time. I move to a back door and open it. Inside the car I find the lever that once pulled allows the back seats to fold down. I pull the lever and leave the seat free of the catch. I quietly close the back door then move back to the boot. For a beat I freeze, hesitating. I force the doubt down then myself inside the boot, into the empty space. Without a handle to close the boot properly I have to pull-slam it shut. He noise echoes inside.

Once again I am squashed into darkness. The phone, turn off the mobile, it could ring. I pull it from my pocket and silence it. Dogs. What if they bring sniffer-dogs here? My scent could reveal me. I could be running, I could be free, but that is what they expect of me. And now, what now? Nothing, just wait. How is this a good idea? I could be running free, but instead I am trapped. All I can do is think, remind myself of where I am, the darkness, the increasing lack of fresh air. I have handed myself over to fate. I must fight these thoughts. Fear was youth and ignorance. They will not take you; they will not take you away!

I hear a car, the sound of a car fast approaching. It stops aggressively somewhere close-by. Doors open then slam shut. A man's voice calls out.

'Round the back!'

The silence returns. Then the sound of people approaching comes from all around. The rub of heavy coats. In my mind, I see uniformed police rushing towards me. Voices call out.

'He can't have gone far!'

Correct.

'The woods!'

'Wait for the helicopter.'

Body heat. Thermal imaging. Am I safe in here? Surely better than dogs? The sound of people moving towards me. A voice, one of the CID Officers.

'I'll drive.'

Followed by the voice of someone new.

'Are you sure you're not concussed?

The front doors of the car are opened. The car bounces on its shock absorbers as people take their seats. The doors are slammed shut. One of the CID officers speaks.

'You alright?'

No reply, nothing verbal anyway.

'Bastard! We'll get him! Fuckin' twice over!'

The engine ignites and we drive away. Finally, I have movement and pace, all of which feels good. Sometimes I desire stillness, need it in fact, but here, now, it is movement I crave. Lying here, in the fetal position, I start to feel calm, even secure. Does the position induce a subconscious journey back to the womb, where all was right and peaceful? Maybe it's the sense of movement mixed with the feeling of invisibility. I love to feel invisible. Once I was afraid of the dark, until one night, I thought fuck it, let the worst happen. Let whatever you fear come and do its worst. After all, fear may shout, 'you can't see them in the shadows', but so what, neither can they see you.

The car picks up speed. We have left the country lanes and hit the A-roads. Twenty minutes to the nearest town. With a fair amount of success, I try and empty my mind, to think of nothing. I see no point in trying to formulate a plan, as my vision into the immediate future is a black as my ride.

Twenty five minutes into our journey, and the car slows to a halt. The handbrake is pulled, and the engine is killed. The CID officer speaks.

'Right. Let's get you looked at.'

The front doors open and the officers climb out. The doors slam shut, and footsteps hurry away. The car alarm beeps with activation; remote central-locking has secured the car.

With their footsteps fading, I push the backseat forward then pull myself into the back of the car. Slowly, carefully, I lean up and look through the side window. Before me stands the local hospital. The two officers are hurrying towards A&E. I wait for them to enter the building then make my move. I open the door and set myself free.

I walk calmly away from the car. I need a plan. A place to hide, to study my only clue. Or maybe I should seek distance, continue to run, to get as far as way as possible, away from the public gaze. How long before my story goes public?

I walk through the car park. Anger starts to fuel me, anger at the people who put me here. I had my routine; I had my peace and now, all is chaos, all is unknown. I want solutions. I want answers. I need to hide. There is too much light. I hurry towards the Out Patients building. I have been here before, visiting, saying goodbye, silently of course. I know a place where I can sit in peace.

As I enter the building, I slip off my rucksack and carry it by hand. This, I think, makes me look less noticeable and helps push me into the background. Several CCTV cameras watch me. Does this matter? Will the police suss my escape and review the footage? Could they? Would they have the time? Maybe later, tomorrow, but today, I doubt it.

I enter the building. It is busy with people. It is nearly noon and morning visiting hours are due to end. No one seems to pay me attention. I glide pass reception and hurry along a corridor. Reaching a door, I take it and enter the Men's Toilets. I go straight to a cubicle, shut the door and lock it.

I am alone, hidden. My surroundings are warm and spotlessly clean, as they say, it could be worse. I push the toilet seat down and sit. From the rucksack, I take out the laptop and boot it up.

Waiting for Windows to load, I almost feel guilty. Here could be access to a life I have no right to view. Twice in my life I have had the option of reading someone else's secret diary, and twice I chose not to. Does that make me boring, too good to be true? Did I refuse to read because I feared the truth? Or maybe I didn't care enough for the people whose diaries they were? Mind you, neither diary left me unharmed. I tore from each a dozen or so random pages, which I later destroyed by fire.

Windows loads, and I begin my search but quickly find nothing of any consequence. No pictures, downloads, nothing that reveals the essence of this woman. Is the computer new? Or barely used? Has it been tampered with, cleaned of vital information? Maybe she missed the techno curve and now only uses computers under protest, if so, I sympathize.

Finally, I find two files that interest me, which could possibly contain the information I seek. The first is a Word document named Draft 1. I do not have the time to fully investigate, but it seems she was writing a novel. The first line of which reads:

'You can take the man out of the cunt, but you can't take the cunt out of the man.'

The second file of interest is an email conversation between the woman and her son, which reads:

"Oh what joy. Welcome to my past - a place I had easily forgotten until you felt it wise and correct to remind me. Well, speak to me, dear mother. But let me warn you, I am no longer the weakling. I no longer see the world through the eyes of a child. You tracked me down. This shouldn't surprise me; after all you are not without some intelligence. I should thank you for my genes, Professor. Nature or nurture? Obviously both. So thank you for the genes although nurture, not you! Anyway, how are you? How well have you aged?"

"Oakley, my son, thank you for your reply. It means so much to me. My health is fine, of course, as my doctor tells me, my cholesterol and blood pressure could both be lower, but what the hell; I have no intention of fading away whilst making up the numbers in some care home.

I have recently retired to the countryside – genuine peace and quiet, although perhaps a little boring. I have plenty of time to think and read, maybe too much time to think, never enough time to read.

I would like to meet up with you, at the very least speak to you on the telephone. I know we have our issues and perhaps, in some ways, I can understand the way you have chosen to isolate me from your life, but can we now at least be civil to each other? I would like to speak to you, is this possible? Can I call you?"

"No. Email only."

"Then email it is. How are you? Are you happy? Speak to me. Tell me where you have been, what you have achieved, tell me your life. Is there family?"

"Life is great. There are challenges and fights. Thankfully, I work towards a time when the challenges and fights have all been won. Science is our only hope, and I am a scientist. I have no family."

"You have me. You're a scientist, of course, what else? Your passion. Your brilliance. I knew you would be. You work away from academia, can I ask why? You had so much promise. I looked for papers published by you but found nothing. This surprised me. What is it you research? I would be interested to know. Your cousin Reese, remember him? I am sure you do. You were once as close as brothers. He is soon to marry and would love you to come to the wedding. Can I tell him you will?"

"My work is secret. I have fulfilled my promise and more! Tell Reese, no. As close as brothers? For a time yes, but then you sent me away. Ask him about Newnham. Were we close? Never. The law is for cowards."

"Why do you still hold what happened against me? On one level, I can just about grasp your feelings, but on another, dare I say it, it all seems so insignificant."

"The butterfly flaps its wings.....My mind is tuned to the future."

"You were sent away to school. You won a scholarship. Wasn't it for the best, for your intellectual development? You had a mind for science. Is what we did so wrong?"

"No. It was for the best. I left, we parted. Simple. There is no big issue here. I do not need a therapist. You sent me away to school. Initially, I hated it. Fear and abandonment etc caused by you and by father, but then settled by me. I found solace in my work. I grew beyond you. Learnt to live without you. Evolved and adapted. It takes a lonely man to see, or rather feel, truth. Think how the gods walked alone from the desert. Get over me. Move on with your life. I wish you no harm, but then again, I wish to share no more of my life with you."

"I see. Then let me say this, when I read your words they made me feel that you are far from happy, contented or fulfilled. You have no family; this pleases you? Who are you professionally? Wasn't the world going to know your name indeed to celebrate your achievements, to owe your legacy a debt? You told me your ambitions, and they were far from fantasy. Many expected you to achieve whatever you set your mind to. So why have you walked away from them?"

"I work for the private sector, and this offends you. You were, are, a crusty old socialist albeit one who sent her son to be privately educated.

Suggestion, grow up. Engage with the real world. Mother, the idealist, well so am I. However, you won't access my idealism in a library. I am totally committed. One day soon, you will see. I will visit you and inform you of my work, of all my many achievements. You will see my wealth and the power of my influence. I will tell you everything, which will result in us parting for good. This is now inevitable. I find your emails distracting, a nuisance. Stop them. I will be flying (by private jet) into the country soon enough. A member of my staff will soon be in touch."

After this I find two separate emails from Oakley, without any reply from the woman. The first email reads:

"New plan. Will call you."

The second:

"Educate yourself. Permission will follow."

The words "educate yourself" have a website link attached. Placing the cursor over the link reveals the web address, https://boxxx5481422.com/oakley. This is the same, or similar, to the page on her laptop, that night I first broke in. Did it show his work, his science?

Families, how they fill your life with joy. These emails, this straw to grasp, are these all I have to go on? They contain nothing explicit, but still, I could do worse than follow the stench of power and money, both of which would have been needed to set me up.

The son, you are now a suspect. Can I get to him? No. All I have is an email address. I could test him. Let him think I have evidence that proves his guilt. If he thought I did, then surely he would try and get to me, and in doing so, prove his involvement.

Her son? Come on, never, it's ridiculous. But it's all I have. Anyway, who else, what else? What enemies can such a woman have?

I need access to the internet. The laptop has Wi-Fi. The only place I know where I can gain Wi-Fi access is the local library. Do I take the risk? Of course. What other options are there for me to take?

I pack the laptop away and make my move. I step out of the Toilets into a flow of people, visitors all rushing to leave. The pace is good, brisk, but then no one healthy ambles slowly away from a hospital.

I reach the exit, step outside and quickly see two options. A queue of female pensioners waits patiently to board a bus, which will take them into town. I could join them, or I could go alone in one of three black cabs, which are waiting in line for a fare. I choose the cab.

I reach the lead taxi, pull open the back door and climb inside. The driver, a woman, which is bad news as she'll remember my face more clearly, turns to look at me. Gently rubbing my throat, as if it was sore to the touch, I mouth the words 'can't speak'. I then point at the hospital then back at my throat. She gets it straight away.

'Lost your voice. Oh well,' she says.

I nod my head.

'Is it contagious?'

I shake my head.

'You can't give it to my husband then?'

I fake a smile.

'Where you going? Here, write it down'

She passes me a notepad and pen. I write "railway station". Taking back the notepad and pen she smiles.

'Right, the station it is.'

I recline in the seat and try to look ill, too weak to enter into any form of communication verbal or otherwise. She starts the engine and pulls smoothly away. It should be a ten minute journey maximum. She spies me in the rear view mirror.

'You look like you could do with some rest.'

I nod. She smiles then looks back at the road. For the rest of the journey, I am left in peace. I try and think of only my immediate objectives, to get to the library and send the email, the contents of which I write in my head. My focus, however, is fallible, and other thoughts push in. I see myself, the image of me labeled and condemned. I think of the driver, her beat of fame, her picture and the headline, "The killer was my fare."

I have never got angry at people who have thought ill of me, never felt disrespected by an insult or a so-called dirty look, and this in Britain where a flash of violence can spring from an eye-line crossed. But by tomorrow, the ill thought that people aim at me will cut deep, and I will feel more than disrespected. I will feel, in part somehow guilty. I can feel it now, guilt stirring anger; a feeling that I am contaminated, that inside me rises unease.

A sharp left hand turn taken too quickly snaps me from thought. We have reached the railway station. As the driver pulls up directly outside the entrance, I hurry to pull a ten pound note from the money belt strapped around my waist. It is money I saved for an unknown time.

'Right then,' she says, as she turns to face me. I pass her the money, smile and nod then move to exit.

'Do you want your change?'

I glance back briefly and shake my head. She smiles.

'Thanks. You get well soon, hey?'

I open the door and hurry out.

Since she brought me to the entrance, I feel obliged to enter through it. I told her the railway station as a precaution, as I didn't want to give my true location away. I walk through the sliding doors and up to a timetable pinned to the wall. I stand pretending to read it until the taxi pulls away. Once clear, I hurry outside. The library is only a minute away.

On my approach to the library, I pass through a small courtyard area where cycles can be parked. I scan the half dozen or so cycles present, but all are securely locked.

The library is barely active. More staff than punters. I locate the Wi-Fi area, sit at a table and read a leaflet explaining how to connect. It seems easy but then technology always does. CCTV watches me. Ten minutes later, I have a connection. I open the woman's email, and the Inbox begins to fill with Spam. With the email from her son opened, I click reply and write:

"You set me up. I know this. The evidence is mine. You killed your mother. I know the truth. I still have the mobile phone, call me."

With the email sent, I try and open the link attached to 'educate yourself', but all that opens is a box requesting a password.

The temptation to search the local news, to see how much of a story I am, briefly comes and goes. I must get away, and quickly.

As I hurry into the courtyard area, I see a teenage girl, about seventeen years old, dressed as some sort of part-time goth. She has her back to me and is unlocking a security chain from a mountain bike. This gives me an option, a choice I can't refuse. A quick look around confirms our solitude. I rush towards her and strike, a single punch to the back of her head. She flops to the ground, semi-unconscious. I take the bike and cycle away. It makes me think, how far can I go?

Exercise, or rather physical activity, always clears my mind. I cycle hard and think of nothing. I know where to go and how to get there, into the countryside and high into the hills. To a place, that tonight, may offer me sanctuary. To a small, isolated chapel nestled discreetly between two villages, a chapel, I believe, will lay dormant tonight.

CHAPTER SIX

Once again I am hiding, waiting in woodland, in a dense, man-made plantation of coniferous trees. Fussy, near parallel rows, planted for maximum yield, act as a prison keeping light and life out. In the distance, I can see the chapel. It is the perfect watch tower, high in the hills and providing a clear and honest view of the only road that leads to it.

As darkness beds-in, the chapel remains empty. Leaving the bike behind, I make my move. I scramble out of the woodland, over a puny wire fence and on to a narrow country lane, which provides a steep incline to my destination.

The chapel is a simple late Victorian building surrounded by its own burial ground. It is brick-built and stands small yet purposeful, with a contented poise. Its proportions are natural and inoffensive until, that is, you notice the single floor, concrete extension that has been flung onto its rear and continues to stick. On each side of the original building are two large, arched windows, which I happen to know have been double-glazed. The congregation who worship at the church is a group called The Christian Fellowship. A notice board outside proclaims, "As in Heaven on Earth." Oh well, I think, there's always hell.

Gaining entry is easy - a single hard kick against the arched, wooden door. Inside it is cold and dark. I feel against the wall for a light switch and quickly find a row of four. I flick one on, give my eyes a second to adjust then rapidly scan the room to form a mental picture of all I see. Once complete, I return the room to darkness.

The chapel seems more a village hall than a church. No pews, just a dozen or so rows of plastic chairs all aimed at a small stage, which is backed by a single blue curtain and a large wooden cross. The pulpit is basic, a lectern in the shape of a cross. I see nothing else that tells of God or worship.

From my pocket, I pull my torch, turn it on and head for a door that stands to the left of the stage. Through the door I enter the extension. I see tables and chairs and children's paintings pinned to the walls. In one corner, I find a small kitchen area consisting of a small fridge, a gas stove, a kettle with jars of tea and coffee, and two Calor gas heaters.

After coffee and a torch-lit hot dinner of baked beans, sardines and two chocolate bars, I settle for the night. My bed is a row of four chairs positioned next to the window. This gives me a clear view of all that approaches. For warmth, a Calor gas heater works fine.

Outside all nature is dark, no moon or stars to burst the night. The only constant light is a single, distant street light, little more than a dot, which marks the approach to a small hamlet called Hope.

A car speeds towards Hope. Its headlights dazzle and snare my gaze. A vehicle-activated road sign spews rich red and amber light, flashing at the driver to slow down. It fixes my stare. Light that cuts through the darkness is always seductive, even more so when you are alone. It's the promise of something, of people and of life.

I should sleep but can't, too much fuel burning in my veins. I turn on the mobile phone and check for missed calls or texts. No one has called or left a message. All is silent, as once I liked it.

Needing to be occupied, I pull the laptop from my rucksack, boot it up and open the Word document containing the novel. I read the opening line:

"You can take the man out of the cunt, but you can't take the cunt out of the man."

A voice in me wants to argue with this, but another, mutters, 'why bother?' All I can muster is this, survival was never easy. I scroll down to the final pages and find what seems to be a story-within-the story, tilted Bunker14382. It reads:

"In the bunker lived the cream of society, the most successful and the most renowned. There were scientists, artists, wits and intellects, all those that could be found, collected and stored before the missiles came to shatter the earth.

Of course, military and political personnel also shared space with the country's finest, as did some from the Civil Service, but even so, the average IQ was still a mighty 165. Men, it will come as no surprise, were dominant. Not in number, but in power, they ruled. Still, there were plenty of women, in fact, more than enough to go around.

Amongst the inhabitants of the bunker the shock of the destruction dissipated with remarkable ease. A new day, a new dawn seemed the only accepted attitude. Billions of people had been lost, but history had been saved, and our culture stored to rise again.

One such inhabitant, Karl, who had previously considered himself to beyond blessing, now considered himself to be the luckiest man alive. Granted, there weren't that many men alive, but still, he concluded, for the first time in his life he was actually going somewhere positive.

Karl, you see, should never have made it to the bunker. Before the war, he worked as a lowly removal man. He was the man with the van, no job was too small, and most were too large. His route to the bunker was a simple case of mistaken identity. Put simply, the man with the van lived while the most brilliant physicist of his generation was left to cower under a table or doorway until his flesh was smashed into a billion or more atoms.

'Can I breed?' Karl asked Major Miles Robertson, whose reply was simple.

'No.'

'Not even a little?'

'No.'

'Why?'

'Resources are limited.'

'So what am I gonna do?'

'You'll cook for us.'

'I can't cook.'

'Can you use a microwave?'

'Yeah, a normal one.'

'Can you read?'

'Of course.'

'Then you have all the skills required.'

'To cook.'

'To cook, and clean. You must, of course, keep the kitchen clean.'

So, it was agreed, Karl became the cook. Nothing fancy of course mainly food that was dried, processed, and microwavable, but nonetheless, Karl was the man who fed the elite, who offered them nourishment and sustenance.

From the very first day, Karl loved his new job in fact he thought it the best he had ever had. Soon, he began working with flair and passion, especially when working at the only real cooking, the making and baking of bread. This simple process of adding salt and yeast to flour and water, then kneading, proving and baking the dough, quickly began to fascinate him. It sustained him as much as the food he ate, as much as the company he kept.

As for the other inhabitants, the top flight anyway, they all seemed to stall even though there was plenty to keep them occupied. They could watch all the greatest films and many of the worst. They could lose themselves in the vastness of a digital library that offered a near endless choice of books and music and of course they had each other for company, laughter and song. There was time for leisure and time for work, yet no new art was created, no new stories committed to type. The military had nothing to guard or to fight. The politicians all agreed. The artists soon became depressed, the wits bored and bad tempered, and the scientists, well they all seemed to go mad with anger and fear and a need for God. Karl, however, stayed level and content. Until, that is, Major Miles Robertson invented a plan. He came to believe-"

No other words appear beyond this.

I look towards the window where a beat of light catches my eye. From beyond Hope, I see a vehicle slowly emerge. It crawls along the A-road until turning on to the single-track county lane that leads to the chapel. The shape of the headlights looks familiar. They certainly sit higher than those of a standard car. It is definitely a four-by-four. But the Land Rover? The vehicle stops. It is now fifty or sixty metres away. I ready myself. Shut down the laptop and pack it away. Sliding the rucksack on to my back the mobile phone shoots out four sharp raps of high pitched sound. I grab it. I have a text message. Read? Of course.

'Are you in? I want to confess. Answer my call.'

I return my stare to the headlights. The phone rings; I answer.

'Sam? Say nothing if it's you,' speaks a voice which is male, well spoken and smugly amused.

I see the headlights flicker. Something, or someone, has crossed the beam.

'So you know my guilt. I cannot deny it; indeed I will not. I made the request, and someone listened. One of many followed my orders. How you know, I have no idea, but then, neither do I care one jot. In fact, it pleases me that you do know. It pleases me that someone innocent knew I was capable of such deed.'

Again the headlights flicker. I assume the worst. They've found me, tracked me down. How? The phone. Their phone. It must have been tracking me. The headlights go dead.

'Anyway, time to say goodbye, Sam. Enjoy the rest of your futile-'

I discard the phone, think for a beat then act. I block the view from the window by pulling the curtains shut. In need of light, I reach for a switch and turn it on. At the Calour gas heater, I pull my knife, find the gas supply hose and cut it in two. Butane gushes out. I move to the second such heater and do the same. At the gas cooker, I open the oven and grill doors, then turn all knobs to full.

Pacing away towards a second window, one opposite the first, I grab a roll of kitchen paper and a tin of beans I had left out for my breakfast. Gas now flavours the air. I reach the window, open it and quickly climb out. Outside, I push the window shut then wrap the tin of beans in several layers of kitchen paper. I could run, but can't, I must stay. If they enter the way I did, into the extension, I have a chance.

I take out my cigarette lighter and ready myself to act. The not so distant sound of a single dog bark alerts my hearing. In the distance, a helicopter flutters towards me. Another sound but closer, the chapel door thumped open. Surely now, only seconds to see the chapel is clear, to find the extension and enter. I ignite the kitchen paper. The flames cut through the dark and spill into my thoughts. Am I ready to kill? To light the fire that burns to death? Through the window, I see the door kicked open. Phillip and Andrew burst in, handguns aimed and ready. As their lungs take the first hit of gas, their bodies recoil back towards the door. I am primed and ready to throw, but something in me forces inaction. Phillip looks at the window and sees me. I act without hesitation, I drop the fuse, turn and run.

I know where to go, into the trees, the thick, dense plantation. After jumping a fence into a field, I face a hundred metre scramble up a steep, grassy incline. Through the darkness, I make good progress, feral-like, as my hands and feet propel me forward.

Behind me a dog barks. The bark is constant, a single, repetitive snap fuelled by adrenalin. The dog has been released, and I am its prey. My only option is to match it as the hunter, so I stop, turn and face the darkness. At least I have the high ground. From the sheaf, I pull my knife. The barking stops. In the sky, the flutter of the helicopter is now a rumble. As bait, I cast my left arm out; the dog duly bites. A furious pain coils deep within. As a release, I stab the knife deep into the dog's back. A sad, even pathetic yelp leaks out. I confirm the kill by slitting its throat.

Suddenly, I am under a spotlight. The helicopter has trapped me in a beam of dazzling light. I hear a bang and feel a force whiz past my face. Instinct kicks me down, and I cower. I see the dog - a muscle packed Alsatian. I snatch it from the ground and hurl it over my shoulder. With it covering my back, I continue my race to the woodland. Several bullets rip and tear into the dog's body. Possessed with a will to live, I quickly and frantically reach the trees.

As I stumble into the woodland, the canopy slices through the beam of light and a thick, smothering darkness renders sight useless. I drop the dog, my shield, and move by touch alone. The only valid direction is upwards, so I continue to follow the incline.

The helicopter loiters above, but machines are not men, they cannot run on empty. They are what they are and nothing more. Helicopters run out of fuel, guns out of bullets. Nothing can inspire a machine, no fear can fuel it.

I continue for twenty minutes or more then pause for breath and thought. The helicopter sounds increasingly distant, and nothing on foot seems to pursue me. A pain throbbing in my left forearm starts to nag me for attention. I ignore it. I pull out my torch, turn it on and continue on my way.

The Woods at night always take your mind to somewhere ancient. Even a cold, hard cynic like me can fool himself into thinking that man is not his own worst enemy. That somewhere, submerged in the shallows of the darkness, lurks something that force alone could never defeat.

Leaving the Wood behind, I emerge onto a deserted country road. A signpost at a crossroads confirms the familiarity of my surroundings. I am high in the hills and need motion, more than my legs can provide. I think for a beat, and remember a nearby farmyard and the beaten up Land Rover Defender that ferried old man Gittins over field and road. It has been a while since I labored for him and his family, but in the world of Mr. Gittins, nothing retires early and by early I mean living, neither man or machine.

I reach the farmyard, and all is still. The nearby house is sleeping. The Land Rover is positioned as if left to aid and abet me, no gate to disturb, no dog guarded zone to violate. I open the unlocked door, lean in and release the handbrake. A gentle push rolls the vehicle silently away. With the aid of a gentle downhill gradient, we soon cover eighty plus metres.

To start the engine, I employ the only useful, practical skill my dad ever taught me, how to hot-wire a car. As an army trained mechanic, he knew all about engines. He used to boast:

'If it's got wheels and an engine, I can drive it, and I can steal it.'

Once, I asked him if that included a jumbo jet plane. He didn't answer but slapped my face for being a cheeky little shit.

The Land Rover shudders alive. I select first gear and drive away. But to where? I need shelter, a wash and rest. I need to think. I need a plan. I do not concede the fate others wish to impose on me. I know a house, isolated and unoccupied. One that is close, maybe too close to the cottage. An empty house near to the murder scene, am I being a fool? What is the etiquette of a man on the run? Flee far away, or prowl close to the crime? What do the police think of me? Have I been profiled? Do they know the house? Do they know I was due, this week, to work there? Do they have the knowledge to second guess me? No! Because they have got me wrong, very wrong! In all their calculations, I am a murderer, which is something I am not!

The thirty minute drive to the house is more an ordeal than the hour spent running through the woods. Driving at night on clear roads creates a sort of stillness, and I do not have the mind tonight for stillness. I become agitated and tense. The pain coiled in my forearm springs into life, and a wrap of cold comes to sit beneath my clothes.

Has the taxi driver taken her bow? The lack of police activity makes me think she has. As I reach the house, I should still be weary, but instead sweep boldly into the driveway.

The house is a nearly finished new build, a six bedroom pile to retire to. My labour was helping landscape the gardens. The owner, Jon, himself an outsider, has often provided me with work. On holiday with his partner, Pam, I was to come and fill a skip with rubble and waste. A good day's labour, one fairly rewarded with money and also trust. He left me a key, hidden of course. I was to check all was well with the house; I was to help myself to tea and coffee, and any food left in the fridge.

To hide the Land Rover from prying eyes, I park it behind the garage. With the house key retrieved from the designated loose paving slab, I rush to the house and enter. Once in, I kick off my pre-planned routine. In the utility room, I strip naked, put all my clothes into the washing machine and activate a quick wash. I then move upstairs to the bathroom. From the medicine cabinet, I find a packet of ibuprofen and swallow three tablets. The wound to my left forearm doesn't look as bad as it feels. Thirteen puncture wounds, some no more than dots, others centimeter cuts, all joined together with the onset of bruising.

Next I take a shower. Hot, steaming water, a luxury that only yesterday would have meant nothing to me, but here, tonight, as warmth seeps slowly into flesh and bone, feels absolutely vital. For a few minutes, I forget my situation and think of sweet nothing.

My planned routine had not accommodated having a shave, but for some reason I feel I must, so do.

Drying myself, I feel clean, warm and ready. Once dry, I plaster my left forearm in antiseptic cream then dress the wound in a bandage.

Downstairs, I pull from my rucksack a change of clothes and put them on. In the kitchen, I hydrate myself with a two large glasses of water. I then make a mug of coffee, which I take, along with the laptop, into the sitting room. Here, I turn the gas fire on to full, sit on the sofa and boot-up the laptop. But for the flames of the fire, and the light emitted from the laptop, the room is dark.

I know the house has Wi-Fi. It takes a few minutes experimentation but eventually I get a connection. I check the Inbox but see only Spam.

Oakley, where to start? I Google him, first just his name then his name plus scientist but find nothing of interest. What else do I know about him? He has a cousin, Reese, who studied at Newnham with him, which is what? According to Google, it's a college at Cambridge.

I go to friendsreunited.com and search for Reese. I don't know his surname, but I know his aunt's surname. Luckily, it seems they match. Reese Robertson left Newnham in 1993. No description just a listing. I search for Oakley, but he isn't listed. This gives me an idea, pretend to be Oakley and create him a listing. Give old friends, if he had any, a means to get in touch, to talk about the old times and what they have heard he's been up to. I could even contact people direct, "remember me, that freak of a scientist? Just murdered my mother. Why don't we meet for lunch?"

Reading the terms and conditions, I see that having joined as Oakley my details will be emailed to people listed in all relevant categories, so I add to Oakley's listing, "wanting to hear from anyone who knew me. Still trying to find myself. So tell me, who was I? What do you remember about me?"

Maybe I could contact Reese, pretending to be Oakley. Speak of the tragic news concerning mother and aunty. Too out of the blue? For now, yes.

How did the woman track him down? Maybe all she got was an email. No physical location. He claims to be a successful scientist, but the internet gives him credit for nothing. His work is secret and for the private sector, so maybe the defense industry.

What was his motive? Why would he kill his mother? Simple, he's a twisted fucking psychopath.

I Google his email address. It brings up no results. On Facebook, he has no listing, so I create him one.

Once finished, I navigate to the website of the local newspaper and see that my story, or part of it anyway, would they ever print the truth, is front page news, "Pensioner found murdered. Local man sought." That's the first time I've been referred to as a local, so that's what it takes.

I put the laptop on to charge then stuff my clean, wet clothes into a tumble dryer. With the timer set for one hour, I move back to the sitting room and sit on the sofa, silent and still.

I could have killed tonight. If I had, then what? They would only have been replaced. At least I know what my pursuers look like now. Let them think I am weak.

Slowly, I sink into sleep.

CHAPTER SEVEN

6.18 a.m. I wake without drama, peaceful and soothed. Remaining still, I strain to capture all sound but hear only the ticking of a wall clock and the gentle, swirling hiss of the gas fire.

I stand, pause for a second then rush upstairs where I scan the view from the front and back windows. The only beat of concern is a helicopter that is speeding my way. This concern quickly flatlines as the helicopter's blue and white paintwork becomes clear. These colours reveal it to be neither police nor pursuers but a helicopter from the flying school at Portmand Airfield. Such helicopters cross the local skyline all day long. The local landscape of hills and coast is considered ideal for training pilots.

This poses a question, would my pursuers base their helicopter at Portmand? I answer yes, why wouldn't they? Where else for somewhere to land and refuel? I refuse to think too much so quickly make my decision.

I rush downstairs and hunt for food. My quarry is two frozen meals taken from the freezer, a fish pie and pasta dish in some sort of tomato sauce. As they cook in the microwave, I pack my clean, dry clothes into my rucksack, put on my boots then go looking for keys. I know a brand new Golf is parked in the garage, and I need to replace the Land Rover, which no doubt is already reported stolen. I find the car keys, both car and garage, dangling from brushed chrome, wall mounted key hook rack.

With the laptop connected to the internet, I check to see if anyone has replied to me as Oakley, but no one has. Checking the Inbox, I see nothing but Spam, so I click on New Mail and, off the cuff, compose a note to Oakley.

"Not speaking to me, Oakley? Why the silence? Trying to deal with your failure? Let me say, you are a gutless piece of futile shit. I repeat, you are a gutless piece of futile shit. I am one, you are many, and still you fail!! Why kill your mother? Was it because she didn't want to fuck you? Did she turn you down you ugly, perverted freak?! It takes a lot to get me angry but let me assure you, when we meet, you will feel the full force of all my fury. I've been saving it up for many years. Didn't know what for, but now I do, for a gutless piece of futile shit, named Oakley. Meet you soon, Sam."

I click, Send and feel an empty sense of satisfaction. Words, for now, are all I have.

Packing the laptop away, I gulp down my breakfast. All I taste is salt.

Once finished, I clean my mess, slip on my rucksack then exit the house. After locking the door, I return the key to the paving slab. I then unlock and open the garage door, reverse the Golf out and replace it with the Land Rover. With the garage door locked, I post the garage key through the letterbox, get back in the Golf and pull quickly way.

CHAPTER EIGHT

I know little of Portland Airfield. All I know is its general location, buried deep in the countryside, and its use as a helicopter flying school. Driving there, I take the quickest, most direct route. Once I twist free of the country lanes, an A-road takes me most of the way. The road carries few other vehicles, but even so, a thin sense of paranoia teases me. I pull the sun visor down to cover my face and argue with myself over the speed I should drive. To speed or not to speed? I play safe and keep within the limits.

Nearing the Airfield, I notice that a short but broad hill overlooks it on one side. I decide to drive there and reccy the area before making any move closer. A single lane road takes me to the top of the hill and a small, unoccupied lay-by. I park, pull the binoculars from my rucksack then scan the view of the Airfield.

The Airfield covers an area of sixteen or so hectares. Cutting through well trimmed grass fields are three runways, all intersecting each other and all at least eight hundred metres in length. A public road borders the entire perimeter, and I can see no security fence housing the Airfield in. Away from the runways, and to my left, I see two large hangers. A three metre high, wire security fence and gate hem these hangers and two acres of land in. Parked on this land are three helicopters, all of which have the familiar blue and white livery. On a field, fifty or so metres in front of the security fenced area are parked two single engine planes and one helicopter. The helicopter is painted matt black and has a thinner tail and a more bulbous cabin than the training helicopters. Away from the runways, and to my right, I can see a car park area and two single story concrete buildings. Signs reveal one of the buildings to be a reception and teaching centre and the other to house a visitor centre and café. Attached to this building is a public toilet. In the car park are parked three average family saloons and the Land Rover Freelander.

Dotted around the airfield are a dozen or so derelict buildings all of which seem to date from the Second World War. People are scarce. I can see only one man who, dressed in clean overalls, stands outside one of the hangers talking into a mobile phone.

Hearing a car approach ahead of me, I drop the binoculars and twist my body round to face the backseats. Here I pretend to fumble around for something lost. As the car passes, I twist back and return my gaze to the airfield. Movement by the café immediately catches my eye, so I raise the binoculars and take a look.

Stepping out of the café are four men, Phillip and Andrew and two others who are unknown to me. The two unknown men could be brothers. They share clothes, attitude and presence. Their clothes differ only in colour, khaki or stone combat trousers, safari shirts and sleeveless tracker jackets, all of which could have been ragged-rolled by the African bush. Both stand a solid six foot tall or more, and both give the impression violence is always the easiest option. Their skin is bronzed and their hair fair. The English countryside feels too small and too tame for them. Give them a big game hunt or African coup to join and profit from and each would seem right. Andrew and Phillip look quaintly middle-class and painfully English beside them. The four of them start talking; Andrew takes the lead. The conversation doesn't appear to be friendly banter rather business talk between work colleges with issues to resolve. Within two minutes, the issues have been tamed. Phillip and Andrew turn and walk sharply away.

The rumble of a tractor approaching ahead of me penetrates the car. Once again, I twist to the backseats and fumble around. With the tractor passed, I re-engage the binoculars and continue to watch.

The Land Rover speeds towards the exit. The two unknown men continue to stand and talk. One of them glances at his wrist watch then casually gestures with a flick of his head towards the café. Are they going back in? I focus the binoculars on their footwear. Both wear stone coloured walking boots. The boots step out of frame. I zoom out and watch as they both enter the café.

I start the engine and pull quickly away. I drive casually into the airfield and head straight to the car park and reception area. I park the car in a parking bay and scan the area for CCTV or other prying eyes. As far as I can tell, I remain unseen. I exit the car and walk purposefully away. With my head down, I quickly pass the reception and café buildings. Reaching the Men's public toilet, I pull open the door and enter.

Inside I am alone. Straight ahead of me stand four sinks, to my left five cubicles and to my right six urinals. The door behind creaks shut. I enter the middle cubicle, shut the door and lock it. Here I wait.

Ten minutes passes, painfully. I struggle with thought. The urge to flee is strong. The need to see some sort of horizon nearly drags me away, but I force myself to stay seated and contained.

The sound of the outdoors blows in followed by a forceful cough, a short, sharp sniff, a man spitting and a door creaking shut. I kneel on the floor and peer through the gap between door and floor. Standing at one of the urinals is a pair of stone coloured walking boots.

I stand, pause for a beat and ready myself for violence. I flush the toilet, unlock and open the cubicle door. Ahead of me stands an unknown. Will he look? Of course not, not in the men's toilet. I rush towards him and smash the heel of my right palm into the back of his head. This thrusts his head forward until his forehead cracks into the wall he is facing. With my hand latched on to his hair, I yank his head back and knee him in the kidneys with all the force I can muster. I then smash his forehead back into the wall. My left hand pulls out my hunting knife and holds it against his throat. I then wrestle his limbering body into the cubicle where I throw him seated onto the toilet. Fifteen seconds of silence and recovery. I watch his strength and senses return. He looks at me and the knife, then smiles.

'What are you going to do, kill me?' he asks.

His accent is South African, his tone, mocking. I place the edge of the blade against his right cheek, pause for a second then whip the knife away slashing down into his flesh.

His whole body tenses and I can see him fight to repress any verbal release of pain. He presses a hand against the wound and looks at me with absolute hate. The situation could quickly explode. In the briefest beat, I see a twitch that tells me the man is about to fight, to roll the dice for all or nothing. I make the first move. Moments later, he is slumped over the now broken toilet, bloodied and unconscious.

I skim a hand through all his pockets and find a wallet and mobile phone, both of which I keep. As I turn to leave, one final action comes rushing to my mind. I locate his right hand, which is lying lifeless on the floor, then stamp on it. Trigger man or pilot, he's out of a job.

I exit the toilets and walk to the Golf with a false air of calm. Once inside, I start the engine and pull smoothly away.

As I leave the airfield, I get a sudden need for distance, to drive many miles away. I have no specific location in mind, but instinct tells me I should head south, to the pull of London. If Oakley has a presence in England then surely it touches the Capital. It should also be noted I hate cities, I hate crowds, I hate people swarming around me. This is something the police should easily uncover and from it conclude that I am likely to remain in the countryside, which I should, but won't.

When alone, I rarely feel lonely, but in crowds I often do. Where there are few, you will rarely go unrecognized, where there are many, you usually do.

What is my objective? To clear my name? To find out why Oakley killed his mother? Then what? Protest my innocence? Who will listen?

The miles ease blankly by, and the fuel tank draws empty. I turn into a passing petrol station and position the car to drink its fill. Security cameras scour every angle. All I can do is pull my up collar, dip my cap and keep my stare dangling towards the ground. I fill the tank with exactly sixty pounds of fuel.

As I walk across the forecourt, I keep my head lowered, and my stare dipped towards my wallet, in which I pretend to rummage for the right amount of cash. Reaching the entrance, I glance over the newspaper stand and half expect to see my face and my moment of fame but, nationally at least, I remain a pre-fame nonentity.

Inside the so-called mini-supermarket, two men are queuing at the till. Taking their money is a miserable looking, over-weight, teen girl who for some reason looks angry with embarrassment.

I take a detour around the shopping aisles, waiting for the men to finish their business. As soon as they do, I pace towards the counter, head down, turning to look with fake interest at the useless products and end-of-aisle special offers I pass. Catching a glimpse of the girl, I see her stare is as rooted to the floor as mine. Reaching the till, I push three twenties across the counter and flash the girl a smile. It misses her, as she doesn't care to look. I turn and quickly leave.

As I climb back inside the car, the phone and wallet catch my attention. Could the phone, like the other, expose my location? I'm sure it could, but why would they add to it such a device? To protect their men? Simply because they can? Ignoring the risk, I turn it on, and as quickly as I can, note down all the phone numbers that have been called or received, as well as those stored in the phone book. Checking the text messages, I find only one, which reads, "Better than Aids!" Attached to it is a photo, I open it up and instantly recoil in shock. The image is a close-up of a black man: his skin is primed with a glutinous sweat, and torn with sores, beacons spewing pain, his stare rages horror. The colour image defies a sense of a diseased, medieval hell. Does this mean anything to me? More sickness?

I turn the phone off. Unable to take the risk of keeping it, I remove the SIM card, as this could contain useful information. I then open the car door and gently slide the phone across the ground. Let somebody find it and keep it on the move.

The wallet, which is anonymous, black leather and seems brand new, yields two hundred pounds in cash and a single corporate, platinum credit card. Although the credit card shows the Visa emblem the card issuer is unknown to me, a bank named AST. The name embossed on the card is Gordon Morkot, below which is embossed GGG Corp LTD. Is this who they work for, Gordon, as well as Oakley?

A batch of five cars pulls into the station one of which eyes my space. I start the engine and continue on my way.

The motorway, like modern air travel, is theoretically a good idea, but in practice it is dull, tedious and sweaty with congestion. The promise of speed is rarely fulfilled. Hell, if there is one, is not a destination; it is an endless commute through an endless rush hour. Most people would fail to comprehend how poor a life I would lead before joining the commuter class. Up and down the motorway, dead in time and pointless in space.

My planned destination is the nearest service station. I don't know for sure, but I guess such a place will have Wi-Fi.

Why, when we have so much choice does it seem we are always in a state of compromise? Here I am, chugging along at thirty miles per hour, caged-in and unable to change lanes. I have made a choice and from it there is no escape. Historically, of course, I move like a God but here, amongst the automotive soup, I feel my whole body is being stamped on, restricted and contained. But for whom, for the good of what? The herd, must we all be a digit in the herd.? Is no one allowed to roam alone?

To my left, I see a channel with a clear horizon - the hard shoulder: arrogant and vacant, smugly guarding its unused space, like some arsed-up aristocratic landlord, utterly appalled by the thought of trespass. How dare it. I swerve left and accelerate hard away. I know the risks but cannot find room to care. Car horns shout and blare. Stares of hate no doubt lynch me, but in ten minutes I am back on the carriageway proper speeding along at seventy mile per hour. Twenty minutes later, I reach my desired location, a motorway service station. As I cruise down the slip road that leads to the car park, I see a sign that advertises free Wi-Fi.

The car park is only twenty or so percent full. It goes against my instinct, but I would prefer there to be crowds of people, thick, dense crowds to become lost and anonymous in. I park as close to the main building as I can. I do this in the hope of catching the Wi-Fi signal whilst remaining in the car. I pull out the laptop and turn it on. As it boots, I scan my environment. The only point of interest is the mass of road markings that cover the tarmac. In one sweep of my stare, I count seven zebra crossings. Official walk zones, marked with thin yellow lines, dictate where it is safe to walk. Give way markings are crammed in at every opportunity. White arrows and yellow zigzags demand something, but what I don't know. Am I safe to leave the car? Is this the watering hole of the stupid, or maybe the government is communicating with aliens.

I try to connect to the internet but get no signal. I will have to enter the building. With cap tilted down and collar up, I exit the car and hurry away.

I enter the foyer. All seems calm, even lazy. The foyer is a hub from which different businesses connect. The Wi-Fi zone is in a café. I'll buy a coffee and connect to the internet. A shop window poster tempts me with the promise of a cheap Pay As You Go mobile phone. Does the staff in these places give a shit? Are we as faceless to them as they are to us, passing blobs of matter all wishing to be elsewhere?

The coffee is self-service, so I fill a large cup. Thankfully the coffee is advertised as real. I count out the exact right money and head for an empty checkout where an employee, a young woman, slim, blonde and still attractive in a sexless uniform, stands wringing her hands with a cloth. She looks at me for a beat then returns her stare to nowhere in particular. As I reach the checkout, I extend the hand that holds the cash. She reciprocates, and the money is exchanged. In a flick of the eye, she sees all is correct. She then throws me the briefest of smiles and returns her stare to nowhere is particular. Another silent transaction. I walk away and take a seat that exposes by back to the largest view possible. There is a handful of people who share my space, but none can see my face.

I pull off my rucksack, remove the laptop and take five minutes to connect to the internet. Checking my new email account, I see I have two new messages, both from Friends Reunited, both telling me, or rather Oakley, that Jonathan Walmsley and his cousin Reese, have sent him a message. I follow the link to my account and log on. The first message from Jonathan reads:

"Well bloody hell, shock news, Oakley gets social!! So you finally had therapy and it worked!! It's Jonathan Walmsley by the way. So how's life at CGG? I see your ugly mug has improved. A sad day for man. Now even scientists feel the need to take the surgeon's knife. I thought you were all a bunch of autistic twats who really shouldn't give a shit. I'm still in finance but don't believe the hype, I'm still making a bloody fortune!! How's my old house? The one I SOLD TO YOU JUST BEFORE THE CRASH!! You still at 14 Upper Addison? I'm not so far away. We should meet for dinner. When are you next in London?"

The word 'improved' has a link attached to it. I click on the link and a new page opens. As the page loads, I see text which is written in Spanish. I check the domain name, which reads CGG.com, and the top of the page where an emblem featuring CGG resides. Is this their corporate website? On the page, I see seven photos, portraits of men, all posed as key figures in the company. One of these photos, the second in-line, is labeled Oakley Robertson.

I pause in a moment of disbelief. Is this truly him? I move in close and stare at his face. He is smiling broadly, is well groomed, handsome and has jet black hair. His skin looks naturally tanned. He is wearing a suit jacket and tie and, I guess, is aged in his early forties. He seems more an executive than a scientist. If I past him in the street, I might think him a prick. But evil? A man who gave the order to kill his own mother? Something in me struggles to accept. But, of course, this face could mask a killer, and the camera can lie with ease. Evil can look like any of us, even on a good day. So this, it seems, is the man who laughs at my misery. I start to feel hate, start to feel it twitching in my eyes and face. It is not a good look for a man seeking to be anonymous. To calm my thoughts, I open the second email. It reads:

"Oakley, this is Reese, your cousin. You surprise me, in fact you shock me. I have tried to contact you at work, with the obvious need to talk to you, and all I get is your silence. And now, this, on the night we learn of your mother's murder you add your details to friends reunited and ask the past to catch up with you??? What should I make of this? I know family relationships and feelings towards family members can be complicated, but do you care nothing for your mother or the rest of your family? I know the police have contacted you and told you all they can. I also know that you are in the country. If you plan to attend the funeral, then please get in touch. You know my father's details; he is arranging the funeral. As of yet, due to police red tape, no date has been set, but you are officially the next of kin! You should be involved. If I hear nothing from you, then I will assume no further contact is required."

He is in the country. At his house in London? I Google 14 Upper Addison, London and quickly find a location. The house is in Holland Park, West London, an area certainly befitting a man of wealth.

Have I found him? If yes, so what? What power does it give me? Could I pay him a visit and confront him? Maybe, but why, for what purpose? To beat him until he calls the police and confesses? What other evidence could I take to them? Can I afford his lawyers? Of course not, but then, think of vengeance? What if something were to happen to him? What if he was to die in suspicious circumstances? The police would then investigate him. Ask who and why. What was the motive? No sign of theft, just murder. They would investigate his life and unearth his secrets. Am I clutching at straws, sounding desperate? Maybe I am, but then on his orders, I am now forced to live, desperately.

Could I do this? Could I kill him? In theory, yes. I could kill him for me, for all his victims, past and future. I could do it to tame my anger. For the basic need to survive.

I feel an advantage, however slight, but also know this advantage could quickly fail. He could after all contact his cousin for real. They could meet at the funeral. Wouldn't he go? Wouldn't he feel obliged? If I move on this, I need to move quickly. Make the decision and pursue it without doubt or hesitation.

I save the street map to disk, as I do the emails, his photo and the CGG website. I need to move, to drive to London. I have no other turn to take.

Before leaving, I follow the poster and buy myself a Pay As You Go mobile phone.

CHAPTER NINE

London looks in on itself. It watches itself with digital coldness. As it draws me in, the risks I take churn my thoughts. I'm a wanted man on the needy streets of the Capital. Cars and people swarm everywhere, but as a desperate man with little to lose the crowds fail to impact on me as once they did. No claustrophobic twitches or paranoid hunch. The traffic is dense, so I sit back and conform, try to purge myself of free will. I must do what I must do. I must act as a man hustled into a situation he would never have chosen for himself. I kill, but I kill only for food.

Head down, avoid stares, do not react to sirens or car horns blasting. Ignore the clock and think only of my objective.

With the map as a guide, I edge towards my desired location. Eventually, I turn into the street, his street. It is wide and straight, with two long rows of three-storey, plus basement, terraced housing. The houses, put simply, are posh: brown brick, skinned with Empire soot and smoke, with identical doors and windows all of which are dressed with heavy white stone borders and cornices. All is uniform. Houses lined up on parade, shoulders back and chest out. All white is white, the latest, newest white. Even the bricks with their multitude of shades seem to merge into a single, uniform colour. The parade, however, is private, as I can see no street CCTV. The pathways host various trees, which untouched by spring, will provide me little cover. Parked cars edge the road and fill a majority of spaces.

I pass his house but see nothing that confirms his presence. As the street draws to a close, I turn the car round then slip into a side-of-the-road parking space. A street sign warns that all parking is resident only. I take the risk, pull out my new mobile phone and pretend to make a call. I feel obvious, out of place and watched. In a public street, I feel like a trespasser, but then of course I am, and worse, I come here to kill.

My plan is simple but incomplete. I have an objective but no notion of the narrative that will let me achieve it. All I can do is tune my senses to focus on my goal and set the future to no more than a second.

Time stutters by; the street remains still. Occasionally, a car rolls by, but no change occurs, either for or against me.

With twenty minutes gone, a black Jaguar Saloon crawls calmly into the street. Approaching Oakley's house, it rolls to a stop. I grab my binoculars and aim them at the car. A back door opens, and out steps a man who is office dressed in a long black overcoat. As he turns to close the door, I get a clear view of his face. It is the man from the photo. Fact. Pacing up the short flight of steps that lead to his front door, he pulls a set of keys from a coat pocket. In his other hand, he carries a briefcase and newspaper. The Jaguar crawls away. Reaching the front door, he unlocks it, enters then closes the door behind him. And now? What now? I have no idea, but still I pull on my black leather gloves, conceal my knife in a pocket and take from my rucksack a length of nylon cord - cord I use for making snares.

And now? What now? I struggle for a beat until a Hackney Taxi splutters into the street. It stops abruptly outside the second house along. The driver, a slight and weak looking man, hurries from the taxi, steps to the back door and opens it. Out steps Lady whatever. Decision made, I make my move. I pull a roll of gaffer tape from my rucksack and add it to my pockets. I then exit the car and rush to the nearest flight of steps. Once hidden in a recess, I stand and pretend to knock the door. Seconds later, I hear the taxi accelerating away. I turn and hurry back down the steps. Seeing the taxi, I fake surprise, raise a hand and flag it down. As it slows, I step to the back door and enter my ride. Once sitting inside, I pull the door shut. The driver turns to me and smiles. Before a greeting has been uttered, I work a fist into his face, knocking him out cold. Grabbing his flaccid arms, I yank him into the back with me. Using gaffer tape, I gag his mouth, cover his eyes, and then bind his hands and feet. I then take the driver's seat and stutter the taxi away.

The street merges with another. I pass a block of flats under renovation. Scaffolding coats the entire building, several skips and portakabins fill the grounds. I make a sharp turn and jostle the taxi into the driveway. A quick scan reveals no prying eyes, so I park the taxi behind a skip then deposit the driver, with a fair degree of care, in-between a skip and a hedge. Back in the taxi, I head back towards the house.

The street remains still. I drive to the Oakley's house and pull up in the parking space outside it. The noisy diesel engine will, I hope, alert him to my presence. Timing is crucial; I don't want him coming out before I reach the door. I beep the horn. Time to go knock. In the mirror, I check my face is reasonably concealed then open the door and exit.

With head bowed, I hurry up the steps. Reaching the front door, I ring the bell, then pulling off my cap, turn to face the street. A quick look at my watch reveals the time, 4.11 pm exactly. I hear the door open followed by a voice, a man's voice, which is calm and slightly amused.

'You've got the wrong house,' he says.

I turn and look at him. He sees my face and a beat of confusion lights in his eyes. I am recognized. I am known, completely, with certainty - not just a face from an e-fit. This, to me, is Oakley. I lunge forward and shoulder him back into the house. As I follow, time seems to vanish. When it reappears, I am standing in the hall behind him. I have the length of cord wrapped around his neck. He is snared, and I am pulling the snare to choke him, dead. His resistance, I barely notice. My focus and stare burns through space. I block out the sound and the image of my action. Soon a vague choking noise breaks the block but then splutters into silence. His body becomes a deadweight, so I tighten the snare to the limit of my strength then meticulously count to ten. On ten, I release him from the cord; he plummets to the floor, more like heavy cloth than flesh and bone. I look away from the body and glance at my watch, 4.15 pm, a four minute job. I feel strangely calm, a touch unsure, but strangely calm. No pounding heart or gasping breath, but then the need to flee comes rushing in. I step to the door. With a hand on the handle, a paranoid beat forces me to stop and look behind. Scanning the hall, I see it. On a sideboard, I see it. Next to a newspaper and an empty vase, I see it. A framed photo, a family portrait, Oakley, a woman and two young children. I freeze for a second then rush to inspect it in close-up. Can it be what it seems to be? In the emails, Oakley stated he had no family. He lied! But still, I turn to the body and search for an identity. I find a mobile phone and then a wallet. I look inside; this is not Oakley. This is Henry Brockhurst! But he recognized me. Who is Henry Brockhurst? I have no poetry. The only word I can hear in my head is, "fuck!" shot out on automatic fire.

The need to flee reasserts itself. I return his wallet then rush to the door. On the street, my only concern is to get to the Golf. I sense people but pay no attention to who and why. Reaching the Golf, I climb inside and lock the doors. As I start the engine, a surge of panic nearly consumes me. I fight it and force it down. A beat of clarity gives me the sense to turn off Henry's phone. Speeding away, a destination comes to mind, a destination that shocks me.

London on the way out is no less constipated than London on the way in. I need distance and space, but I am stuck in a car that now feels as contaminated and wanted as I am. Guilt and paranoia can quickly strip you of all sense, in fact of all self. You can lose control of your thoughts. Silence can be lost never to be hooked again. I struggle for clarity. I have killed; I have murdered an innocent man. Can I rationalize this? Of course. I mean, I did. I was to kill Oakley and force an investigation, Oakley being far from innocent. But now, what now? I have murdered an innocent man. But was he? Was he an innocent who was randomly selected? Was he something darker? He was rich, no doubt powerful, corrupt even. Follow the money, let the stench lead me to the rot. He knew me. He had knowledge of me far beyond that gained from watching the news or seeing my e-fit in the news. Anyway, would he have the time to care for some countryside murder? Oakley wanted him dead, but why? Was his nose too deep in the trough? Had he served his useful purpose? Oakley wanted him dead, and he rolled the dice that I would do it for him. Whatever the truth, I was set-up. Again,

I am the fool but should I wallow in guilt? Yes, one day, maybe, but now, now I must survive. I must get out of London. My face has gone, or will soon go, national. I am losing. I need to find land. Can I make sense of this?

Why this location? Why is it in my head? Is it weakness? A sickly need for a man I should be able to trust? Am I now not enough for myself? Is like drawing like? Are we now ever more connected? I swore we would never be as one. Maybe anger is demanding a face to touch and to blame. I must be cold, professional. Use him. He is close. Take something back. A night's sanctuary at least. No one would predict I would visit him. He lives close by. Go there. Be practical.

My father murdered my mother. Served time for her manslaughter. I was the star witness, the silent one of course. I have watched him from a distance, but he hasn't felt my presence now for many years. He lives close-by and alone. This is not the time. Never is the time. Why is this in my head? Because I must do what I must do. Will I ever have the chance to see him, or use him, again?

CHAPTER TEN

Reaching Essex, I quickly find a space and dump the car, or rather park it legally in a busy street. In the hope some other thief may steal it and take it away, I leave it unlocked with the keys in the ignition. Dusk is moving in. I've a good four mile hike to my father's house. If anything can empty my mind, it is exercise. I pace away. When the streets are empty of people I will run, when they are not, I will walk.

My father lives on the edge of town, on a small estate of newly built houses. A place for non-professionals who are swimming well with the tide. All the houses are detached and have either three or four bedrooms. None has a front garden, just the largest tarmac driveway possible. I approach his house. All looks well and respectable. A BMW 3 series is parked on the drive. A light behind closed curtains hints at someone's presence. I either walk on by or walk to the door and knock. On an estate like this, a loitering stranger is quickly sussed.

I walk to the door and ring the bell. The door is solid, UPVC and so conceals all action behind it. I ring the bell again. Seconds pass. The door opens aggressively as if releasing a pent-up wave of confrontation. There in front of me stands my father. His eyes dance with surprise, but his body remains firm and unmoved. He is smartly dressed, as he always was, wearing an open neck shirt and tailored black trousers. Physically, he is obviously older but still well-built and unafraid. His face reveals little of his past; it reveals no pain or shame. His stare gives nothing away; he could slam the door shut or welcome me in. Silence binds us. As I stare at him, my hate for him refreshes itself. Finally, with a flick of the head, he grants me permission to enter. I step inside, into a poorly lighted, cold, narrow hallway. As I pass him, my body instinctively twists to prevent our bodies touching. He pushes the door shut. I turn to face him. The muffled sound from what I assume is a television eases our continued silence. Finally, he speaks:

'You talkin'?'

I shake my head. He steps in close and fixes his stare onto mine. On his breath, I smell whisky.

'Did yer do it?'

I shake my head.

'But you still need to run from it.'

Silence. I match his stare, which for the first time in my life seems easy.

'You think I believe yer?'

I shake my head. He can believe whatever he wants.

'I can't believe yer, can I? I can't believe yer, cos I don't know yer. It's been too long. And anyway, you're my son, who knows what a fuck-up you are.'

He laughs, genuinely amused, his stare still fixed on mine. For a second or so he stands, literally laughing in my face until his laugh cuts as suddenly as it began.

'Follow me.'

He steps past me and again my body quietly recoils to avoid having to touch him. He opens a door and disappears into another room. I stand still and silent. The television is turned off. I hesitate, but then step forward and follow. I enter the living room. It is gently lit by two wall lights. The décor and furniture surprise me. New, modern, coordinated furniture and the latest home entertainment gadgets style the room. It all seems rather nice, comfortable and pleasant. I guess he bought the look, an entire page, from some mid-range catalogue. An over-sized plasma television steals the show. There are several framed pictures hanging on the walls, all depicting rural landscapes. I look for photos of people, family or other but see none. He is sitting in an armchair, holding a glass of whiskey and cigar. His posture is proud and arrogant. In front of the armchair, stands a glass surface coffee table on which an ashtray, a packet of cigars, a packet of cigarettes, a nearly full bottle of whiskey, a cigarette lighter and two remote controls all stand. He has seen me looking at the room and is pleased I have done so.

'What do yer think? Alright, innit? What yer think, I'd be livin' in some shit hole? No fuckin' style…Fifty five year old man livin' on his own, can't function. Can't use a fuckin' washing machine. It's all a piece of piss really. I mean, I don't care for any of this, telly excluded obviously, but yer gotta have a certain pride, and as I say, it's all a piece of piss. Buy quality, put it all together with neutral colours and hey fuckin' presto, you have a fuckin' nice room to get pissed in…I should tell yer to take your shoes off, but once in a lifetime, hey? Take your coat off. Sit down.'

I do as he says. Rucksack first then coat, placing them both on a small, decorative chair. He gestures to the second armchair and again, I do as he wishes.

'Well, well, fuck me, my son. Come to visit his old man, hey? But why? This the last refuge of the fuckin' desperate? You think they won't look for you here? Well yer wrong. To them you're a killer, a twisted piece of shit who smashes life out of sweet, old ladies. They'll look for you every fuckin' where….Nice to see you though, hey? Every cloud has a silver linin'.'

He laughs, mildly amused, raises his glass and tips it towards me. His stare constantly sticks to mine. He doesn't trust me. He thinks he knows my motive but can't be sure.

'So, you're here for what? Food, money, drink. Hey? What? My fuckin' support?'

I have no answer, only stillness.

'Jesus Christ, my son. What's it been, fifteen years? What yer been up to, hey? What you achieved? Get a glass. Get a drink.'

I shake my head. The two of us pissed would not be a pretty sight.

'Still not talkin'. What the fuck is the point of that?! Never understood it. Didn't yer wanna shout at me? Hey? Call me a cunt?!'

I am calling you a cunt.

'Or take a swing? That would've been better. Or something worse? Maybe that's why yer here. Come to do your old man, take some revenge. On a fuckin' spree, are yer?'

He forces a laugh. Is he worried?

'Here you are, my only son, and I don't know yer…Who are yer, hey? What have yer become since the last time?…Me? Your father, I ain't done too badly. In fact, been thinking who the fuck am I gonna leave all this to? Y'see, I own this house, every last brick, every last spec of fuckin' dust, it's all mine. Plus money, cash. There's a fair old sum stashed in the bank. Well, banks, actually, seventy five gees max, if you know what I mean? Got shares, too. I've done alright, ain't I? Army, builder, prison, builder, inherit a few quid, buy to let, sell at the right time, retire! Fifteen grand, that's all I inherited and y'know somethin', that's what you're gonna get, from me. Fifteen plus inflation. See how you do, hey? See if you're better then me. Fancy yer chances, do yer? See if yer beat me.'

I already have and it wasn't difficult. Well, maybe until tonight.

'If yer can of course. If you have the opportunity on the outside that is. Gettin' carried away with a bitch of a wife.'

That hurts. It was meant to.

'Ain't the same as what you did, or didn't do. I got out, you, who knows. Fuck, you're in some shit, ain't yer!'

He sips his whiskey through a smug little grin.

'Fuck knows where the rest's gonna go, I mean once you've had your fifteen. I got no one else. Couple of ex-wives but y'know, fuck 'em. They've had enough already. No one else special in my life. What about you, got anyone special in your life? Papers say you're a loner, or loser, both I think.'

I remain calm, exterior view anyway, and I keep my body still. Still, silent and passive. It may sound weak, but I know he hates it. It gives him nothing to feed off.

'For fuck's sake, can't you get a computer voice or something? Y'know, type the words in and let it speak for yer? Cos like this, you might as well be a fuckin' post or somethin'. A fuckin' slab of concrete. It's like, yer not even a man.'

Silence. He fills his glass with whiskey then takes the cigarette lighter and re-ignites the dying cigar.

'I'm smokin' again. Y'know why? Cos I know what death is. I've seen it. Seen it quick and seen it slow, and frankly, when it comes to me, I want it quick. I ain't gonna be one of them silly bastards on the slow train in some old twats home, if y'know what I mean? And what, you gonna care for me?'

Silence. A pause. He looks at me. I sense he actually wants an answer. Is he ill? He doesn't look it. He always had the constitution of an incinerator.

'Wouldn't want it, son. Wouldn't want it. Do me one thing though, promise me this, if I ever go do-lally, y'know senile, or for that matter some sort of fuckin' cabbage, you have my permission to shoot me.'

He laughs loudly.

'Betcha can't wait? I'll give you the fuckin' gun if yer want? Nah, you'd prefer to see me senile, a dribblin' wreck, hey?'

In my time, I've harnessed a fair amount of self control but even I can't silence an ever-so-slight smile that accompanies the thought of my father as a full senile wreck. He sees this smile, and it fuels his hate.

'What's in yer head, hey? What the fuck is in your head? Gotta be somethin' in there. Y'know, you could be a fuckin' psycho! Yeah, a fuckin' psycho! That's all I need. They'll probably blame me. Well fuck you, I'll blame yer mother! I'll sell 'em the truth and you can fuckin' read it.'

My mother, for the record was blameless. We, me and him, are the guilty ones.

'Your wonderful fuckin' mother! You might romanticize her but here's the truth, I didn't mean to kill her, I just wanted to hurt her, and why? I'll tell yer why! Cos she was a dirty fuckin' whore!

The ejector button is pressed. I fly towards him. He stands ready to fight, but in less than a second I have him pinned to the floor with my right hand gripping his throat. I am strangling him, my father, and for the first time I witness in him the fear that he once inspired in me. His struggle is futile. His strength has gone. The physical presence that he once waged so effectively is now barren and old. The only force he has left is his words. Suddenly, I pull my hand from his throat.

'Hurt me! Fuckin' c'mon, yer cunt!'

'No,' I speak.

We pause, looking at each until rage, unable to force its way out through his body comes rushing out through words. I reach for my rucksack. I will tie him up, gag him of course. I will then use any useful resource I can find in his house. Once I finished, I will leave him, alive and alone. I am innocent and have the world to tell.

Even my father has Wi-Fi. I never feel left behind, but now, just for a second, I do. With the laptop booted, I connect to the Internet. The Inbox delivers an email from an unfamiliar address, but one I know has come from Oakley. It reads:

'Thank you, for being both simple and obvious. You made it so easy. Now you are guilty. Enjoy life while you can.'

A reply comes rushing to mind, but nothing virtual, one he will have to feel and physically touch.

I close the email and navigate to ccg.com. The site is down. Only a blank, white page is visible. The site before was a fake. Uploaded with the sole intent of fooling me, which it did with ease.

I Google "cgg" but find nothing of any importance. I add related words, but again, find nothing. Finally, I try "ccg gordon morkot" but still, find nothing. What sort of business is this silent and invisible, this closed to the public? Not one desperate for new customers, or with shareholders to please.

I search "ast", the bank who issued the credit card. The results show them to be a private bank registered in a country called Lichtenstein, a small county in Europe where money goes to loose itself, a no-questions-asked tax haven.

I need a connection. All I have is a fake website. Mind you, fake or not a website still needs to be bought and built. Their virtual fingerprints must soil it somewhere, so I Google "find out who owns website". Selecting the top result, I am taken to a site called whois.net. In a text field labeled "Look up registration details for domain" I type in ccg.com then click a button labelled search. A page opens up. The following information is revealed: the registrant is listed as a company called CV Designs. The administrative contact is Philippe Veirea. An address and phone number is also listed. I Google the phone number; an address in Paris, which matches the one listed, is returned.

I have a name and a destination. Of course, both will be several degrees removed from Oakley, and anyone else who matters, but at least the whiff of a scent has been caught.

I must hunt with caution in fact paranoia. I must assume they know in fact can manipulate the moves I am making to get to them.

Next, I Google the list of phone numbers I took from the South African's phone. Most are mobile numbers and reveal nothing. The one landline number, which was a number called not received, shows itself to be prefixed with the international dialing code for Malta. Further investigation reveals the number to be for the headquarters of a charity called Reach, a charity offering help and advice to mainly African migrants who illegally find their way into Malta. A news article that mentions them reads:

"A migrant flood has overwhelmed the tiny sun-splashed island nation of Malta over the past five years, stirring charges of human-rights violations, taxing the nation's tiny navy and fueling xenophobia.

The rocky archipelago, about 55 miles off the coast of Sicily, is best known as a tourist destination. But the start of summer brings mostly

African migrants, crossing the Mediterranean in rickety overcrowded boats, on their way to seeking a better life in Europe. Boatloads appear almost daily.

'All of a sudden we saw quite a phenomenon; hundreds and hundreds of migrants started appearing in our waters,' said Lt. Col. George Frendo, the officer in charge of Malta's air, land and sea operations.

Malta's embattled government made a fresh plea last week for EU assistance after the military detained another 28 illegal migrants and Interior Minister Tonio Abela warned that hundreds of others were dying trying to reach Europe.

'The situation right now is a complete mess, it's a free for all,' he told his EU counterparts, days after immigrants whose boat capsized were left clinging to a fishing net for three days while Mediterranean nations argued over who was responsible for them.

'For migrants who reach this 122-square-mile outcropping of limestone and medieval fortifications, where more than 1,900 people reside per square-mile and jobs are scarce, the relief of survival is quickly followed by the realization that the journey is over.

Upon arrival, migrants deemed to be from "safe" countries like Egypt or Morocco are immediately deported, but the rest spend up to a year and a half locked in detention centers while their cases are assessed. A controversial charity, called Reach, which has been set-up to offer help and legal advice to the migrants, has claimed treatment of the migrants has contravened European human rights legislation."

Is this connected? Can it bring me as close as the website can? For now, I think no.

Who is Henry Brockhurst, why did Oakley want him dead? I search the London news and find the story breaking. A headline reads "Hedge fund manager murdered at home". The motive for the killing is reported as theft. I Google "henry brockhurst hedge fund" but quickly draw a blank. Not a problem, as surely the press will investigate for me.

Decision made, I must get to Paris. After printing a map of the Paris address, I search the house for extra resources - cash and food. I find and take £450, two tins of tuna and two tins of beef stew.

I leave the house, sneak silently out. Dad, I leave; I don't even grab a final look. I've had my fill. It's business now. If he sees me gone, he'll do his best to free himself. I need time, a good few hours before the police are told of my visit. As I walk away, I conclude to tell no one of his situation, never, ever. He can sit and wait, wait for someone to come. Maybe no one ever will, but then, maybe he needs to witness that.

The sharp night air snaps at my senses. The sky is free of cloud. The moon is full, but the stars barely shine, dimmed by the fog civilization.

How do I get to France? First step Dover, or the surrounding coast. My plan is simple, stupid even, steal a boat and sail there. First though, first I must steal a car.

CHAPTER ELEVEN

Stealing a car, an old one anyway, is easy, but a boat? The journey to the coast has made me think my plan is naive. My knowledge of boats is limited: quite a few fishing trips out to sea, but not once did I take the helm. So can I, the coastal voyeur, the day trip fisherman, win against an angry sea? Can ignorance navigate a knowing tide? Even if I do manage to hotwire a boat, and why would I, I never have before, do I just point it forwards and hope for the best?

I reach a town called Deal. Near the town centre, I park and leave the car. With midnight close, the streets are silent and free. I hurry away and head for the sea front. Listening to hear the sea, I quickly catch its rhythm. Its mood seems contented, at ease with itself. An old friend permits a sliver of hope.

My plan is now one of improvisation, one of need and desperation. I cross the road to the promenade. The sea is only heard, as the black of pure night cloaks it completely. At the edge of the promenade, I look down, and with my torch pointing, punch a hole through the darkness. Five feet below, I see a circle of shale beach. I edge the light forwards and quickly touch the sea. Twenty metres ahead of me, it draws closer with every breath. It comes to welcome me. Now offer me a ride.

With the torch probing the beach, I hurry along the promenade. My plan is simple, with the tide yet to fully return, I will find a fishing boat - one stuck dead on the beach waiting to be revived by the tide. Soon a cluster of such boats is caught in the beam. I jump down onto the beach and head for the nearest. A quick inspection exhausts my knowledge. The boat is made of wood, is about twenty foot long and has a cabin at the front. I haul myself on board and step to the cabin. A locked door blocks my path, so I kick it open. Inside, I pause, confused and lost. My only beat of inspiration is to press every button, which I do, twice. Nothing starts, no engine fires, no instruments shine. Like some disgruntled customer, I turn and leave. I will take my business elsewhere. To the next boat I hurry. Falling from the boat my feet hit the shale and then, nothing, I vanish.

CHAPTER TWELVE

I crawl calmly out of my sleep with a yawn and a slow, growing stretch. I am at peace, lying face down on a vinyl padded seat that runs the length of my body. Reality then enters without knocking. I feel, then see, my right arm chained to the wall. I am a prisoner, and this is my cell. As information floods in, I stand and hone my senses.

The room is small and cramped, the two birth galley of a boat that is steaming gently ahead. A closed door is beyond my reach. The only noise, a low revving diesel engine mixed with the sound of displaced water rushing out of the way. I pull at the chain to free myself but quickly and knowingly fail. My instinct now is simple, kick at the wall. Let my captor hear I live. Let them sink with the cat in the bag. I lash out and boot the wooden hull. It holds, so I kick again with added force and violence. The door flies open. I stare at a man, the Sailor Man. He speaks:

'Is that the best plan you got, son? Well carry on, cos I'm a fuckin' good swimmer.'

He looks at me without fear or even concern. His laidback voice and loose casually held body seem disconnected from his deep, intense stare. His age is mid-forties. Physically, he looks healthy, with a thick-set strength forged by work, not leisure. His face wears the trials of life with a rugged, contented ease. His body surfs the rocking boat, absorbing all movement. His presence commands calm, if not obedience.

'I'm taking you to France. You're paying me of course, but, I know who you are, Samuel Dean.'

Clear, simple information that serves only to confuse me. His accent is hard to define, although hints at an Irish past.

'I knocked you out. A fist for the trespass, then something a little stronger to get you on board and us away. Here.'

He throws me a key, which I clumsily catch.

'Free yourself, but look at me.'

I look him in the eye. His voice seems almost throw-away, but his stare carves his words deep into time and memory.

'Make one move against me, and I promise you, I will kill you.'

I believe him. I trust him. I have no other option. I must live in the seconds.

I unlock the padlock, the chain falls from my wrist. The Sailor Man places my rucksack on the table.

'Your possessions, minus £400, which I've taken as my fee. A fair, honest price, I think you'll agree.'

I nod. He helps me, a man accused of a terrible crime, and he frees me for £400.

'Shall I answer your question?' he asks.

I look at him. What question?

'I'm helping you, why? You! The scum that you are. Well, are you guilty, Sam?'

I shake my head.

'Good. I believe you.'

How can he believe me? No one can read the truth or detect a lie. People think they can, but they can't. If we could, how long would we last?

'Do you believe that? Do you believe I believe you didn't do it? Or do you think, maybe rightly, I'm a man who simply doesn't give a shit?'

I shrug. I have no answer. He smiles.

'Do you think you'll need a weapon, Sam?'

From under his coat, he pulls a handgun, an automatic with a matt black finish. I answer honestly, I nod my head. He tosses me the gun. I catch it with firm, steady hands.

'It's loaded. The safety catch is on, but other than that, it's ready to use.'

More confusion, clogging my thoughts.

'Take it. You'll be doing me a favour. If you don't, the sea will take it.'

He turns and exits through the door. My stare finds the gun. Questions try and enter my mind, but I solidly refuse them access. Forcing action, I put the gun in my coat pocket then grab my rucksack, which looks and feels correct. I slip it on then sit and wait, my stare fixed to the door. After several seconds, without thought or reason, I pull the gun from my pocket, find the safety switch and push it to the off position. The feel of the switch and the sound of the click are solid and somehow satisfying. I return the gun to my pocket, where it and my hand, continue their embrace.

The door opens and the Sailor Man returns.

'All on course. Twenty minutes and you're away on land…Do you know France?'

I shake my head.

'We'll dock out of sight, close to a town called Grand-Fort-Philippe…Do you have a plan?'

I shake my head.

'Good. Improvise.'

He sits opposite me. A small table separates us. He stares at me calmly, without a hint of self-consciousness. Two strangers, men at that, staring at each other in silence. Neither feeling awkward nor needing a prop such as a drink or a cigarette.

'I know France, well. I served in the Legion, the Foreign Legion. Served a full ten years. Not that they take mutes, or murders from across the channel, so don't think I'm offering you an option. I'm just telling you something about myself…I served in the Legion, and other forces. Had a few sticky fingers in a few sticky pies. Some for profit, others not. There's a surprising amount of opportunity out there for men like me, and you.'

Meaning what, I wonder. Who does he think I am?

'Did the quiet life suit you, Sam?'

With stillness, I refuse an answer.

'Silence, is good. Underrated. It's an asset. Look after it…You know, I could've left you on the beach, took your money anyway, but I didn't, you know why?'

I nod as if I know, but I don't.

'Unfinished business.'

He grabs the collar of his shirt and coat, pulls them down and exposes a six inch scar running from his lower neck to his upper chest.

'Unfinished business. Finished now though. Completely dead. Anyway, we better get you to France.'

He stands, pulls a business card from a back trouser pocket and places it on the table.

'Take this, there's a phone number on it. If you're desperate, use it. Send a text. You might find it useful. But only if you're desperate, hey.'

He steps away and exits through the door. I grab and examine the business card. It is a blank, white, devoid of any print. The number on it is hand written in black biro. I have no intention of calling the number, but I keep the card anyway.

The night is calm and peaceful, the sea completely at ease. As the boat brushes against a jetty, I step off and land in France. Once again, I am alone and feeling in control. Having already bid farewell to the Sailor Man, I pace quickly away. Darkness prevents certainty, although it seems a deserted strectch of rural coastline is ahead of me.

The land of France is new to me, but the language I know well. My mother was Spanish. Before she met my father, she criss-crossed Europe working in various hotels. She learnt several languages with ease and passed them on to me. My mother, if only she could see me now, if only she could see the waste.

My plan is simple, steal the first car I can and use it to drive to Paris.

CHAPTER THIRTEEN

I have speed - another stolen car, another mark against my name. The country A-road I drive along is deserted. I am the lone commuter winning and losing the rat race. In the distance, a traffic sign shines, its message, too small to read. I slam on the brakes and screech to a halt. Stepping out of the car, I check to confirm my solitude then pull the gun from my pocket. I have used guns before, shotguns, air-rifles and pistols, all of which seem quaintly amateur in comparison to the one I now hold. It feels darker, more seductive, then any gun I have held before. It fits my hand perfectly; it wears me well. I look to the sign and take aim. I steady my line of sight then firmly squeeze the trigger. A bullet fires and rages towards its prey. All is easy and undramatic, a simple tool for the fearful masses, for me, myself and I.

I pick the spent shell from the tarmac, put it in my pocket then slip back into the car. At the road sign, a bullet hole scores me a kill.

I take the quickest route to Paris. No county or scenic view. I choose the blank, peaceful monotony of motorway travel.

Paris welcomes me in silence. The city is mine. I am alone in the city of romance. It is 4.10 am and the deserted streets guide me effortlessly towards my destination.

The address I seek is in the Paris 3 district, which seems several rungs removed from the chic and glamorous. Not quite the underbelly, but the first stop in, and the last stop out. The narrow streets are walled-in by tall, three to five-storey buildings stretching as far as the eye can see. Rows of parked cars, all pointing the same way, further enclose the space. At the ground floor level, commerce greets the eye, above the shops and businesses, live the people.

I park the car. Dare I call myself lucky? The good chance was mine to steal a small hatchback, which now fits smugly into the only space available. With a tentative pause and mild sense of trespasser's guilt, I exit the car and take my first smell of Paris. All I can say is that today must be the day the bin men do their business. With map in hand, I hunt for the building. The address must relate to an apartment or office, either way, a two door entry. Discreet and stern looking doors stand scattered between the shop fronts. Some have numbers above or to the side, others do not. The building I seek is number 138. I find it and quickly concede to the door, a single, solid wooden slab that is beyond its prime but still sufficient, like an old prize-fighter earning cash to keep the door, its form and reputation enough to keep the peace. Entry is by electronic keypad. It will take more than brute force to defeat it. I will wait for the day, so hurry away in need of air and exercise.

Back in the car, watching and waiting with a monotone focus. Slowly the city opens for business. At 8.15am, I pick up my phone and call the number taken from the Whois information. It rings only twice, then is answered by a man who, in French, speaks calmly and with a professional tone.

'Hello, Philippe Veirea.'

I cancel the call. So he's in, but how to get to him? I realise I know so little. How does he plead, is he guilty or innocent? Is he a stooge or an active player? Will he recognize me? Of course, this could all be a trap, my presence predicted or known. My aim is to get into the apartment and look for clues. My plan to achieve my aim, unknown.

The discreet, stern doors start releasing the workers. A man dressed casually exits door 138. I pick up the phone and call the number. Philippe answers with calm and grace; rudely I cut him off.

Increasingly the street fizzes with people. I start to feel exposed as various stares take time to acknowledge the car and me. A well-built man in an expensive suit enters a café and takes a window seat. His line of sight is naturally inclined towards the door 138. Is this his mission? Does he too watch and wait?

My stare flitters from one man to the next, with the question, does he fit, following closely behind. I touch my coat and feel the gun snuggled in my pocket.

Door 138 flies open. A man, dressed cheaply for the office, dashes impatiently away. I make the call, Philippe answers, still calm and polite. Two young men walk lazily towards the building. Their tired, grinning faces talk of a night to remember. As they reach the prize fighter, one changes his mind, turns and saunters across the road, towards a bakery. I take my chance. A prop would be nice but nothing comes to mind. On the off-chance, I reach into the back of the car and pull the backseat down. In the boot I see boxes, presents wrapped. I stretch further in and pull them out, two large boxes and three smaller ones. The pink, High School Musical happy birthday wrapping paper tells me all I need to know. The tears of a child to add to the list.

I exit the car, open the back door and pile the presents on top of each other. The party guy exits the bakery. In a white paper bag, he patiently carries his breakfast. I pick up the presents and close the door. Held just right they conceal my face. To 138 I hurry. My timing is just about perfect; the race is a draw. He looks at me with a hazy grin, and without thinking, taps in the security code. Seeing the presents he speaks,

'American shit. Kids, huh. Brainwahed.'

I smile in agreement. He pulls the door open and waves me in. Door number one is breached. I enter the ground floor. To press my legitimacy, I confidently head for the stairs and quickly consume the first flight. A casual glance behind confirms the party guy follows. I slow my pace, pretending the presents need more concentration than they actually do. As I reach the top of the second flight, I turn to snatch a glimpse, he has left the stairs for the corridor. Alone, I continue to the next floor, the floor where Philippe resides, but then what? Bang the door, let him open it then knock him out? Too crude, too exposed, for now at least.

The interior is grey and cold. Metal stairs and wooden floors announce every step taken. Echoes wait to trap and return any sound that tries to quickly fade. I stand in no man's land, midway up the third flight of stairs, my stare and concentration flicking between Phillip's door and hunting for signs of people.

Ten minutes crawl slowly by. Plans, or rather hopes, form in my mind. Echoes tell of people leaving, fortunately all from below. The urge to move closer takes me. I reach his door and pass it. At the foot of the next door along, I dump the presents. Stepping back to his door temptation prods me, knock the door and punch him. I resist the act and take my reward, a noise: the flick and slide of a security chain. As I step away towards the presents, my hand grabs for the phone. The door is pulled open. I hit the redial button. A man half emerges from the door until the call of a ringing phone pulls him back in. He spits a word, one unfamiliar to me - my mother didn't teach me to swear. I make a dash for the door. My foot saves the close. Without hesitation, I push the door ajar and slip inside. A small hallway: three doors, to my left, right and ahead. The right door, which is open, leads to a bathroom. I slide inside, twist behind the door and hide. The phone is answered. I instantly cut the call. He spits out the word for the second time then paces out of the apartment. The door slams shut. I pause and listen, anticipating surprises. His footsteps trail an echo down the stairs, through the door and out. Silence. Door number two is breached.

Through the door opposite, I find a small kitchen, which contains no surprises. Through the third door, I enter the main living space, which is a bedroom and living room all in one. The décor is stylish, well kept and precisely placed. The air is scarred by the stench of cigarettes. A bright red two-seater sofa faces a neatly made double bed that is draped in a silky, purple bedspread. The dark wood floor tiles creak with pressure and shine, glossed with polish. The only carpet, which is red, separates the bedroom area from the rest of the room. The only window, which faces the door, is partly covered by wooden shutters. I take a peek though it but see no way to escape. I step to the bed, lift the bedspread but see no space to hide. A home office space - a corner desk, a LCD monitor and computer, a keyboard, laptop, phone, camcorder and printer, fills one corner of the room. Shelves hold various files, magazines and books. Above the door is a mezzanine floor on which stands a single bed, armchair and stereo. This, I conclude, is my only hiding place if needed or interrupted.

What exactly am I looking for? What, in fact, can I find? I have little idea, so I move to the desk. The LCD monitor is on stand-by; I turn it on, and a desktop page appears. With the computer booted, I activate Outlook and watch two Spam emails fill an empty Inbox. In the Deleted Folder, I find several dozen emails one of which, delivered yesterday, reads:

"All details for website attached. To go live ASAP! An hour max. Domain name ggc.com, you registered this for us a while ago. Further instructions will follow. I assume your bank details are unchanged."

I open the attached Word file and see the text and photos used on the cgg website. He built the site and registered the domain name. So what? It doesn't mean he's part of the crime. Who sent the email? I look at the address, a hotmail account, which tells me nothing.

Next to the mouse pad a notepad catches my eye. I see written on it: a Paris address, today's date and the time, 10 a.m.

I look at the other deleted emails. All they reveal, or rather confirm, is that Philippe is a website designer working from home. I have his website and contact details. His clients include a hair salon, a driving school and a tattoo parlor. My instinct tells me he knows nothing about me or the predicament I am in.

And now, what now? Find and search his accounts. He's worked for them before so maybe an invoice exists that could tell me more.

Five minutes into my search, and I have found nothing of interest. Six minutes into my search and a noise heard outside the front door grabs my attention. The sound of metal on metal, a key violating an unfamiliar lock. I switch off the monitor then, taking no chances, rush to, and climb the ladder that leads to the mezzanine floor. As I reach the top, I hear the front door open then quickly close. I pull the gun from my pocket. A space between the bed and wall offers a place to hide. I accept the offer and sink to the floor. The wooden bed frame clears the floor by four inches and allows me a limited, and slightly exposed, view of the living space below. Footsteps sound, coming my way, ever closer. A man's voice, speaking in French, is heard.

'I'm in. He's yours…When I've cleaned up here…No, nothing…Is the eye watching?…How dull…Not my style, mother-fucker…Yeah, you should wish, but give me her number.'

A man enters my line of sight. In one hand, he carries a motorcycle helmet, in the other, a mobile phone. He looks serious, to the point of being miserable and unpleasant. Physically, the weigh-in between us is even. He wears blue jeans, black leather gloves and a black leather motorcycle jacket that looks far too new to be cool. His hair is long and dark; his face denied a morning shave. He places the helmet and phone on the desk, then pulls off the gloves with a strange sense of aggression, yanking at them, as if compelled to use too much force. As he tosses them on to the desk, he snaps his head back and urgently stretches his throat as if compelled to do so.

Turning to survey the room, he casts a contemptuous eye over all he sees. This job, it seems, is beneath him. Catching sight of the notepad next to the mouse pad, he grabs it, studies the top page for a beat then, with a brief, smug grin, tosses it into his helmet. I see his hands are skinned with a pair of latex rubber gloves. Turning the LCD monitor on, he sits at the desk and begins working at the computer.

Clean up? Is this them? Clean up Philippe? Why did he remove the notepad? Have they arranged to meet Philippe at the address? For what? To clean him up? To kill him?

Philippe, I think is a web designer, pure and simple. Why would they need to kill him? Why would they take the risk? For a ruthless attention to detail? To remove all risk? To erase all loose ends?

They think I am coming. 'Is the eye watching?' Watch the apartment on the off-chance. Clean up all evidence, however slight, that connects Philippe with them. Arrange to meet Philippe and clean him up, too?

The man suddenly stands, and with a fuck-it attitude, paces away towards the hall. Decision made; I stand and step to the stereo, which is plugged in and left on stand-by. I turn the volume control to zero then turn the stereo on. An LCD display flashes a graphic that tells me a CD is loading. I aim and ready the gun. Footsteps sound, approaching from the hall. The man, carrying a mug in his hand and an unlit cigarette in his mouth, enters my line of sight. I snap-slide the volume to full. A sonic boom of techno music explodes into the room and pounds into the man spinning him around to face me. Aiming for his body, I pull the trigger: the gun fires a bullet and his face explodes. I cut the volume to zero. I stand, listening. Normality continues. I hear no panic or confusion. I am, for now, unnoticed.

I stare at the kill, its face torn off, its head seemingly gorged by something wild. In this moment of time, I feel nothing - felt worse shooting rabbits. Another link on the chain smashed free.

The need to move rushes in. I slide down the ladder and step to the kill, where I rip the leather jacket from its body. The pockets yield no clues, no wallet or weapon, just a key, embossed with the word Honda, and a metal device, which I guess is a lock pick, both if which I keep.

At the computer, I check to see what the kill was up to. The email regarding the website has been deleted, other than that, what can I know? I check the time, 9.10 a.m. Philippe is due to meet them at 10 a.m. I Google the address. The location is a café situated in a district I passed on my way to the apartment. I study a map, memorizing the directions.

Taking the kill's phone, I search all records for numbers, as I find them I write them down. When finished, I take out my phone and take several photos of the kill in the room. I then create a text message to Philippe:

"You are in danger. The people you meet want you dead. Run and stay away."

I select the photo that will best show Philippe a dead man in his apartment, attach it to the text message then save it to send later.

The motorcycle jacket fits me well. I zip it up, slip on my rucksack then pull on the gloves. I think about taking his trousers and boots but quickly decide no. The helmet is a touch too small, but with a firm pull just about fits.

When Philippe half emerged from his apartment, I saw he was wearing jeans and a beige coloured jacket, but I did not see his face. A quick look around the room reveals a framed photo of, what looks like, father and son. Both look proud and respectful. I memorize his face, then make my move out of the apartment, down the stairs then out on to the street.

Without looking for the Eye or anyone suspicious, I head straight for a motorbike and moped parking zone that I passed on my way to the apartment.

Amongst a row of a dozen or so low rent mopeds and scooters beams a Honda CBR600 sports motorcycle, a beast of a bike, not for the subtle or faint-hearted. Convinced it's my ride, I take it. I climb on-board and take a few moments to acclimatize. With the key in the ignition, I start the engine, which wakes with a low, warming rumble. I've ridden plenty of motorbikes before although nothing as savage as this. Anyway, the best policy when entering the unknown, is to get on with it, just do it and do it quickly. I kick the bike into gear then pull away in character, arrogantly at full arrogant.

A willingness to accept danger can somehow make you feel secure. I glide along the avenues and boulevards effortlessly consuming all in my way. The high level of concentration needed confuses time, and I reach my destination as if pushed through a void.

At the mouth of the street, I pull up and park in an allotted space. Keeping the helmet on, I pace away from the broad, open space of a boulevard and enter a darker, narrower street, more densely populated, street. Locals flow smoothly along, backpacked tourists add stickiness and do their best to clog my path. I pull off a glove then retrieve and ready my phone.

Forty metres ahead, and on the other side of the street, the café comes into view. From it, a single row of tables and chairs has begun to invade the sidewalk. Standing over a table is Philippe and Andrew. Philippe gulps down the final mouthful of coffee a cup has to offer; Andrew looks for something approaching in the distance.

I activate my phone and send the text message to Philippe. Andrew finds what he's been looking for, a black Audi Saloon that pulls up five or so metres away from the café. He speaks to Philippe and points at the car. I remove the helmet, cover my lower face with my scarf then quicken my pace. Philippe pulls a mobile phone from a pocket. Andrew places a polite hand on Philippe's shoulder and guides him towards the Audi. Pinpointing my location with a single turn of the head, Andrew looks at me with a blank, empty stare, without any sense of recognition.

A solid slab of shoulder purposefully rams into me. Turning to make eye contact with the aggressor, I see a man in his early thirties, styled as a clone of Andrew, who meets my stare without fear or emotion. Behind him, two more such clones pace ever closer. In the near distance, sirens sound. I turn and look at the café. In the background, I see Andrew reach the Audi. Behind him Philippe follows, his stare fixed on his phone. In the foreground, two more clones move to encircle me. The sirens continue to draw closer. Philippe reaches the Audi and hesitates. Patting his pockets, he looks back at the table. Andrew opens the back door and returns the guiding hand to Philippe's shoulder. I glance behind; the three clones loiter with a passive-aggressive menace.

I pull the gun from the side jacket pocket and in an instant deliver a bullet into each of their bodies. Pandemonium erupts around me. I turn and hunt the clones behind. Each one crumples to the ground as a bullet pulls them from life. I look up and see Andrew watching, his stare acknowledges me now. He tries to jostle Philippe into the Audi, but with his nerves already fired, Philippe slips his hold and flees. I, too, take my cue and run. I turn and sprint back towards the bike. All stickiness has gone; I now repel all those around me. A glance behind reveals Andrew pulling away in the Audi.

As I reach the bike, I slam on the helmet and stuff the gun back inside the pocket. And now? What now? I start the bike and feverishly speed away.

As my fame recedes so does the temptation to flee the city. Instinctively looking for the familiar, I find myself speeding back the way I came. Nearing Philippe's apartment, I turn into a deserted side street, pull up and park. In the distance, sirens scream chaos. I dismount the bike and walk steadily away. A commercial sized rubbish bin blocks the pavement. I remove my helmet and feed it to the bin. With phone in hand, I type a message to Philippe.

"Stay away from your apartment. They may track you from your phone. Don't trust the police. Soon I hope to explain."

I send the message then drop the phone through a drain, into the solitary bliss of the sewers. Turning into the street that leads to Philippe's building, I watch the people, the shoppers and the café dwellers for any sign of recognition. Fortunately, news travels fast and I, the real story, slip by unnoticed. At the entrance to the building, I tap in the security code, open the door and enter. Running up the stairs, I slip off my rucksack and reach inside for the lock pick. Approaching Philippe's door, I see the presents have vanished. Using the pick, I easily and quickly gain entry.

Inside the apartment, all remains as I left it. I race to the window and peep outside. Nothing I see concerns me. Pacing to the desk, I pull off the motorcycle jacket and toss it back to the kill. From the desk, I grab the camcorder then quickly return to the window. With a watchful eye on the street below, I fumble with the camcorder and eventually get it working. Filming the kill, I test-shoot a few seconds of footage then play it back to confirm all is working. With this confirmed, I place the camcorder on a bedside cabinet and position it to film as much of the room as possible. Next, I remove the laptop from my rucksack, boot it up and connect to the Internet via Philippe's Wi-Fi. As the Inbox fills, I return to the window and see what I thought I would, a black Audi saloon pulling up outside the building. A back door opens, Andrew ejects himself out and fires himself towards the building. The Audi denied a place to park pulls aggressively away.

I rush to the camcorder and press record. I then snatch the laptop, close it and put it in my rucksack. Pacing to the bathroom, I slip on the rucksack and pull out the gun. Inside the bathroom, I leave the door wide open and conceal myself behind it.

A loud, confident knock on the front door. A ten second pause followed by the exact same knock. A five second pause followed by the sound of metal on metal. The door opens then quickly closes. Footsteps pace down the hall and into the main living area. A beat or two of silence followed by Andrew's cold, agitated voice.

'He's dead. We need to clean-up…Because we can! Five dirty, one clean it still makes sense to me…We'll have to take the risk…After the last text, I hardly think he's coming back, do you? Send them in, I'll wait.'

He'll wait, for a team, for back-up? Do I risk remaining unnoticed and filming more evidence, or do I walk away and take my winnings?

Footsteps rap against the floor approaching me but then veer into the kitchen. I make my move; the gun aimed and ready. I creep from my hiding place and position myself in the hall. The kitchen door swings open, and out steps Andrew. Seeing me, he casually comes to a stop. His body remains lose and unafraid. He throws me a friendly smile then starts to clap his leather-clad hands.

'Let me applaud you, Samuel Dean. Take my praise, Samuel Dean. I mean, you're a nuisance, for sure, but a first class fuckin' nuisance if there ever was one.'

Using the gun, I gesture for him to get down on the floor, a gesture he blindly ignores.

'Do you know who we are, Sam? Stupid question of course you don't know who we are. Nobody knows who we are. We are nothing you or anyone else can ever find or ever know.'

He takes a single step towards me narrowing the distance between us to two metres. I'm sure he's had a gun in his face before, and I'm sure he's been trained to fight.

'Justice doesn't seek us. The authorities cannot investigate us. No crime can stick to us. Whatever you think you are initiating, however you think you are progressing, you are deluding yourself. In fact, all you are doing is building the case for your own psychopathic insanity. You, Sam, you, are the killer that justice seeks! We, we are nothing! We are completely unseen!'

I repeat the gesture to get down on the floor.

'No. Shoot me or make me, but I will stand!'

He takes another subtle step towards me. I aim the gun at his leg fully intending to fire.

'Wait!'

He half-heartedly raises his hands just above his head.

'Whatever you want, Sam. I know you mean it. I know you've got the taste for killing. It's easy, isn't it? Hey, now? The taste is sweet now. The first human kill is like acid on the tongue. But now, it's a sweet, tasty treat. So enjoy it, before the blandness, before it gets blander and blander until finally the taste is nothing, it's tasteless, far too easy to swallow. What's your score by the way? How many men have you killed, Sam? Tell me, you could join a club of mine.'

He booms out a burst of quick-fire laughter. Again I repeat the gesture.

'Can't I stand? I'll face away from you. Shoot me or knock me out. Question me, Sam. Ask me some questions. What is it you want to know?'

He turns his back on me. He's stalling, planning something, waiting for his back-up to save him or for a chance to fight me. I pull the trigger and shoot him dead. With the noise of gunfire ringing in my ears, I step straight into action. I search his pockets and find an automatic handgun with a silencer attached, a mobile phone, and a wallet containing euros, pounds and a CCG corporate credit card. I think about discarding the phone but instead turn it off and put it, along with the wallet, into a pocket.

With guns in hand, I pace to the window and take a look outside. An ambulance is parking, at an unhurried pace, in a no parking zone close to the building. Once stationary, two men, ambulance men in uniforms, exit the ambulance, one from the front and one from the rear. The man from the rear hands the other man a large, well packed holdall bag then re-enters the back of the ambulance. A few seconds later, he re-emerges carrying a light weight portable stretcher. After closing the rear door, they stroll towards the building. The indicators on the ambulance flash twice to show the doors have been locked remotely. Is this the clean-up team? I assume it is.

I stuff my gun into my belt then, removing my rucksack, pace to and grab the camcorder, which I turn off and place inside the rucksack. Slipping the rucksack back on, I return to the hall and open the front door, leaving it slightly ajar. I then drag Andrew's body into the main living area and dump it next to the Kill. Finally, I dash back to the bathroom where I stand hidden, examining Andrew's gun. Seeing the safety catch is enabled, I turn the switch to the off position.

The front door creeks open. A man's voice quietly speaks,

'Go.'

Bodies rush into the hall and pass the bathroom. I step out and see the ambulance men about to leave the hall and enter the main living area. I aim the gun and pull the trigger. Another two men are pulled from life. The silencer does its job well. I search their pockets and find a vehicle key. Putting the gun in a pocket, I head for the door and exit.

In the corridor, all is still. I close the door and pace quickly away, down the stairs and out into the street, where sirens continue to swirl and wail. People stand together talking, but none show alarm or concern for a gunshot heard. As I reach the ambulance, I remotely unlock its doors. A quick glance around reveals no prying eyes, so I open the drivers door and climb inside, into my carriage, my ride to free me from the city.

A part of me wants to burst into laughter. I breeze through the city with barely an interruption. The sirens repel all in my way. The laughter, however, remains untapped.

Having cleared the city, I pull up into a lay-by. My next move is undecided. Am I any closer to Oakley? Have I stepped towards the truth? Unable to think of an answer, I pull Andrew's phone from my pocket, find the correct button and turn it on. Expecting it to ring, my stare loiters on its screen, but I receive only silence for my time. On the screen, an icon catches my eye, a message unread? I navigate to the inbox and find a message from someone called Spitz. It reads:

"Remember who you answer to. We may be one, but we are not the same."

Is this important? I discard the phone on to the dashboard, take the laptop, boot it up and check the emails that were uploaded while in the apartment. They are all useless spam. As I snap the laptop shut, Andrew's phone sizzles into life vibrating with an in-coming call. I grab the camcorder, turn it on to record, and then bring it to the phone and my ear. I answer the call and hear the calm, self-satisfied voice of Oakley.

'Sam?..Samuel?..Silence…Then let me assume it's you…Sam, all this fuss, all this drama and complication. You want me, well here I am. Let me give you my address; let me tell you where I am: Sea View, The Mount,

Mgarr, Malta. I repeat, Sea View, The Mount, Mgarr, Malta. The biggest, whitest house you can see from the village. I'm here now, at home. It's a beautiful day. Clear blue skies and a crisp, blue sea. Visit me. I have a funeral to attend in a week or so but until then, I am all yours. I will clear my diary for you, Sam. In fact, either you arrive within 72 hours or, on the hour, every hour, someone will die... Who? God knows. Just some random man or woman, selected somehow, from somewhere. No one important or close to you. Just another average human being found to be clogging up the earth. Some will welcome it, others will not. Anyway, there it is. Simple. You want me, and now, you know exactly where I am. See you soon, Sam.'

The line goes dead. I stop the camcorder recording, rewind and check to see if his voice was captured. It was. Nothing conclusive, but still, I have another link fixed to the chain.

He's done well, a good move on his part. They want control and that's how to do it. The bastards. Give me a destination. Make me predictable. I saved Philippe, so what; they think this is my weakness? Give me a timeframe, achieve it or we will prod you where it hurts. Is he there, probably, I mean, why not? What risk is it to them? All the risk is mine. I must rush there risking exposure and capture from the police and whoever. And anyway, how do I get there and more importantly, how do I leave? Malta is an island close to the middle of nowhere. Where can I run, where can I hide? Even if I get there, they know I'm coming, all they have to do is wait and plan. But I want him. I want him to see me, to smell me. I want him never to forget my greeting, or for that, my departure.

Weakness, have no weakness. Rationalize it all away. Create your own morality. Blame the greater good. To kill on the hour, every hour. Would they? Who the fuck are they? 'We are nothing you or anyone else can ever know.' Well, how true is that? How much of them are Oakley? Do they stop with him or go well beyond him? Would they really kill as they promise to?

Control, they control me, but I must fight to keep the lead ever slack. I should disappear and wait. I should remain unpredictable. But then, what wilderness is left to accommodate me? This is the wilderness. Live or die. Never find peace.

It was never going to be easy. What is their weakness? They don't expect to lose, and mine, I don't laugh anymore. In my favour, I could never survive prison. Do I have an advantage? Surprise. I get there fast, impossibly fast. My only chance is speed.

Andrew's phone is state-of-the-art, one of those new smartphones that are starting to become desired. I fiddle with it and soon get it connected to the Internet. I search for and find the website of my local newspaper. The headline story is an interview with Oakley. He's made an impassioned plea for me, the killer, to give myself up. He is described as the broken son, who after years of separation, was starting to rebuild his fractured relationship with his estranged, but loved, mother. He will attend the funeral and will fly in from his home, in Malta.

Seventy-two hours. I will visit him. No more virtual communication.

Using Google Maps, I memorize a rough route then turn off the phone and accelerate away.

CHAPTER FOURTEEN

The E15 Autoroute tumbles by. The ambulance and its siren shield me from the crowds and cut me through the tollgates. Seven police cars cross my path, none of which care to notice my presence. My plan is simple, drive through France and Italy and make the short crossing to Sicily then hire or steal a ride to Malta.

Two hours pass and my thoughts remain focused, without drift or indulgence. Four hours pass and the sagging fuel gauge breaks my cocoon.

A road sign directs me towards a petrol station. I pull up and park by the air hose. Of the three cars parked at the pumps, only one is being filled. A tanned, slim man, drenched in expensive arrogance, and still fresh in his twenties leans nonchalantly on a BMW M6. With pump in hand, he lovingly satisfies its thirst. Once quenched, he returns the pump, closes the petrol cap with a delicate twist, then saunters away to pay. His hands are empty, and the car remains silent. Are the keys left in the ignition? The ambulance has served me well but is damaged goods and will offer no advantage when driving through Italy. Opportunity or risk? A theft that will be far from subtle, but if speed is my main objective.

I scoop up my belongings then scramble out of the ambulance. With little attempt to conceal my intentions, I pace to the M6 then peer though the driver's side window. The key dangles from the ignition. I open the door and slide inside. With a twist of the key, I ignite the engine, then bait it with a dab of the throttle. Provoked, it roars a warning of its power. Without looking to witness the wrath of Mr. Whoever, I drop the accelerator and burst towards the exit.

Two hundred and fifty miles separate me from the Italian border. Do I continue ahead using the fast, free-flowing Autoroute, or do I opt for the slower, but probably less policed, minor roads? Again, I choose speed so continue on my way.

The M6 does its job well, although I barely exploit its potential. Speed in such cars is a gimmick, a paper asset, a never to be realized boast.

The miles ease by and my focus, aided by a good dose of paranoia, stays lean and tight. Police cars come and go. Some rush past, while others seem to stalk me for miles.

I leave France and enter Italy with zero resistance. The motorway carries me seamlessly and should continue do so all the way to *Reggio Di Calabria*.

Trapped in hours of constant speed, I barely feel as if I move at all. I've been driving now for ten hours straight, and my resolve is grating thin.

Tiredness has started to worm its way into body and mind; my senses are becoming muted. As the miles stack-up, one on top of another, the curtains close, and the road funnels me into darkness. A trickling stream of dazzling headlights serves only to highlight the monotony. I should yield to sleep and hunger but fight and resist the urge. I must stay hungry to keep the hunter awake and ever moving forward. The car takes its fuel and carries on regardless. I stutter into sleep then pulse back awake. I've taken fourteen of the seventy-two and can no longer fight the urge. In a service station car park, I lie back and think of nothing.

Should I be able to sleep this well, after the day I've just departed? A dreamless, instant sleep as if thrown into shock. For three short hours, I feel nothing.

I bolt from sleep and wake without transition. Turning off my watch alarm, I see the time is 3.15 a.m. Tiredness still threatens, but for now, has been contained.

Back on the motorway, and my path is clear. I test the M6's potential and slash away distance. The paper asset is made physical, and a boast is earned for another day.

With the time approaching 7.30 a.m. I enter Reggio Di Calabria. Close to the port, I dump the car, rush the remaining distance on foot then catch a ten-minute ferry to Sicily.

On the ferry, I am nothing but a tourist, seen and noticed only when necessary. I stand on deck leaning on the rails with my face held and caught in the morning sun. I sense nothing of my surroundings or the people around me. I have no mind to admire scenic beauty. The sun is to mask my face with a tan not to soothe me with its warmth. Approaching the port of Messina, I feel nothing of its history. My desire is the modern, the cranes and the terminals, for the efficient dispatch of people.

I leapfrog Sicily with a taxi ride from Messina to Pozzallo. Solid, quality sleep is made impossible by a driver who reels off a history of everything we pass. I tune him out and sort of semi-doze my way through the hour-long journey.

In Pozzallo, I skim the seafront and marina looking for a backdoor into Malta. No opportunities seem immediate, so I flock with the tourists and take a hydrofoil that will get me to Malta in ninety minutes flat. The time is 9.45 a.m. and from the seventy-two, twenty-three have now been spent.

I start the crossing locked in a toilet. I'm not sure why, but I do. So far my face has gone unrecognized. Am I wanted for Paris? Is my face international? If so, no one is rushing to grab the reward.

Tired, I try and sleep, but fail. The air is too hot and stale, the rush of water too loud. I need fuel, water and food. The only food I have left is a tin of tuna, the only water, the half bottle remains from a litre bottle bought from a petrol station. I consume them both with a feral speed. The water serves only to tease my thirst, likewise the tuna with my hunger. I could reccy the hydrofoil, look for refreshments and breathe fresh air on deck, but decide to stay locked and hidden.

Time, sometimes you wish you could piss it away, other times you wish to hold it locked in your arms forever. My time, now, is as sticky as the air that lies dead in these stinking bowels.

Finally, an hour dies. I make my move. My landing needs to be invisible. With the toilet empty, I leave the cubicle and make my entrance out into the hum of people. The space that holds us is one of those generic commercial spaces, could be a bar, restaurant or cinema.

The only direction I want is down. A wall sign takes me to the stairwell, and the stairwell takes me to the vehicle deck, where rows of tightly parked vehicles provide alleyways for me to scurry along. Several men in uniform and high visibility vests mill around chatting, none has the mood to be bothered by my presence. I walk confidently, as if I know where I'm going, which I don't, all I know is what I'm looking for, a speedboat I watched towed onboard, one protected with a mooring cover. My plan is simple, for the cover to hide me as well as the deck.

I find the boat and make my move. The cover is strapped tight to the boat, too tight to allow me entry, so I loosen two of the ratchet held straps just enough to give me the room to slip beneath.

Back in darkness, in the fetal position, lying in a puddle of tepid seawater that has been contaminated with a generous spill of engine oil. The air is warm and tight, breathable for now at least. Will the driver notice the loosened cover?

Occupied by every sound that comes my way, time quickly passes. Soon the hum of people is swelling around me, a wave of slamming doors and firing car engines. A gentle bounce tells me my driver is seated and ready to go.

Again, I have motion. I look at my watch and illuminate the time, it reads 11.07am. At quarter past, I will make my move. The motion is start-stop for a minute, becomes smooth for three then returns to and remains start-stop.

With the eight minutes dead, I take my knife, stab the blade through the cover then slash a cross a metre in length and width. Clear blue sky dazzles my vision, and my ears fill with the sounds of an urban road. Without looking to fully assess my surroundings, I make a pact with me, when the vehicle next stops, I get out and run. Seconds later, my ride begins to slow. As it stops, stationary for a second, I burst out through the cover. A split-second reccy reveals a congested, narrow urban road, and shops, cars and people all hustling for space. My ride is pulled-up waiting, as a rubbish truck bullies its right-of-way. Gambling against collision, I leap from the boat into the middle of the road. A burst of adrenalin induced speed saves me from the truck. For several seconds, I sprint aimlessly through crowds of bewildered people until the sight of a narrow side street gives me direction.

The side street swoops upwards and proves an invigorating climb. It is dead straight and a good hundred metres in length. Its leathery cobbled surface shines as if polished for a parade. Ragged, stone-built, four-storey buildings, soaked in and stained by history, enclose it on either side. I see no people, behind or ahead of me. For a moment, the only signs that people exist are the caged birds left out on balconies which sprinkle the air with song.

The side street deposits me into another near identical street. With people now in view, I slow my run to a walk. I need speed, to be faster than man. I decide to find my way back to the tourist swells and look for a taxi. The grid street plan soon provides a channel back to the coast. Once breached, I merge with the crowds. A taxi sits queued in a row of traffic. I make my move, I tap on the driver's window and gesture for a ride. An enthusiastic nod grants me permission. I open the backdoor and climb inside.

The Driver requests a destination. I take my notepad and I write, 'Mgarr. Can't speak. Operation on throat.'

Seeing my words, he replies,

'Sure. No problem. Mgarr.'

Accelerating away, we overtake the boat owner who, parked up on the side of the road, angrily examines the damage I caused.

The journey time is used to ready the guns. Keeping them hidden in the rucksack, I remove the silencer from Andrew's gun then place them, hidden and held in my trouser waistband.

Twenty minutes later, I am alone and on foot, hurrying away from the village Mgarr. It is 11.50 a.m. and from the seventy-two, twenty-five have been spent. Is this good? Enough to deliver surprise?

The address should be no more than a mile away. Ahead of me is a dusty, deserted road that stumbles its way through farmland. Small, thirsty fields, some alive with crops, others stripped bare to soil, roam upwards from a valley floor. The midday sun poses with menace; my cap counters none of its rage. Luckily, my thirst for revenge shouts louder than my thirst for water. Forcing myself into a gentle run, I push against the midday heat.

Half a mile nearly felled. In the distance, high in the hills, I can see what I hope is the address: a large, gleaming white house that stands as the lord of all it surveys, bejeweled with a swimming pool, open and unprotected, single-storey to arrogantly consume an extra slice of the precious land, its too few windows, squinting and undersized. I take my binoculars and zoom in for a close-up. I see no people or cars in the driveway in fact nothing to indicate that anyone is home. I pause, hesitate for a second. I was fooled once before, but still, cannot resist the urge to move forward.

Another half mile fully consumed. The home-straight beckons. A narrow, single-track lane, barely fit for a car, leads me to a steep, persistent climb. The route is open and exposed. My only cover is distance aided by the dazzling sun. As the incline plateaus, the dry-stone wall that borders the lane pauses to offer free and easy passage on to the grounds of the house. Without hesitation, I take it.

The house and I stand exposed, facing each other. The mainly paved, shadeless ground between us is manicured and decorated with lush, potted vegetation. Apart from my gasping breath, the only sound I can hear is the gentle trickle of lightly falling water.

No cameras, staff or security. No sense of company, if anything, a sense of quick and sudden desertion. Dismissing a thought to reccy the perimeter, I hone in on the front door then rush towards it. As I reach it, I pull and ready a gun.

The name of the house is emblazoned on the door in bronze wire letters. I grab the door handle, twist and push. The door opens; once again, free and easy passage is mine.

I burst inside into a spacious, open-plan living area. The walls are white, the furniture regal and the air chilled to a shudder. All looks clean and barely lived in. Three closed doors offer me hope that I am not alone. As I step forward, I see a newspaper, the Malta Times, lying on the stone tile floor. It has been placed front page up and positioned square against the door for someone, me, to see. The headline screams, "Plane Crash Tragedy" and four photos of four men leer at me from the page. The first is unknown to me, the second is Phillip, the third is the South African and the fourth is his colleague. I swoop down and grab the paper. Underneath the first photo, is written the name, Oakley Robertson. I speed through the story - last night a private jet flying from Malta to London crashed into the Mediterranean Sea. Cause unknown. The crew of two, and the two passengers, are all believed dead. Oakley, described as a scientist and hedge fund consultant, was flying to England to attend the funeral of his recently murdered mother.

He's dead! Now? Dead? Never! No! Dead?

In my hands, the paper feels thin. I snap it open and find the front page of the Paris Gazette ablaze with the headlines: "Massacre on the Streets of Paris. Five random men gunned down. Local man is sought". A section of text, highlighted in yellow marker pen, tells how three witnesses heard the gunman speak with a Parisian accent. I turn the page and find another loose page, again from the Gazette. A small, buried story, highlighted to catch my gaze reports how Philippe Veirea is dead, found hanged in his apartment, a suicide. To the final, bastard page, The London Times, and the murder of Henry Brockhurst. The police seek two men. The motive they claim was robbery. Valuable items are missing from his home.

All is clear. I stand innocent. They've cleared my name. Well let me confess. Let me speak the truth!

How? Why? Silence. Cut dead! He's dead, so where now for me? Still no explanation, still no reason why. A plane crash, maybe. An accident, no. But why? What was I getting close to? Something bigger and beyond him? What did he risk exposing?

I drop the paper. What now for me? Silence? Keep moving, keep looking.

I feel small, suddenly intimidated. Pushed, squashed by a dense, dark hidden force. Keep moving, keep looking. I look around for something, anything. Look in draws, cupboards, all empty with the everyday. A post-it note stuck to the fridge, which reads:

"All clean. Carpet will have to wait but new vacuum due Tuesday. Rosemary."

I scrunch it up and throw it away.

I pull out Andrew's phone and turn it on. Let them speak to me! Will they speak to me? I get the thought, check the internet, and prove the stories are true. As the phone logs on, a throaty, menaced groan born of great effort sneaks up and startles me. Instantly, I point and aim the gun at the source, hidden and unidentified, behind one of the closed doors. For a second, I freeze but then burst free towards the door, which I boot open with a desperate, angry kick. Inside, I find a bedroom: curtains closed, room light on and Oakley. Oakley, is this him? He is strapped to a stiff, straight-backed, near throne-like dining chair; his face is torn with agony; his mouth vandalised with sticky, semi-dry blood and heavy, black bruising. I step closer to him. He looks at me with hate blasting from his eyes. Am I to blame? His forearms are strapped to the arms of the chair. His hand's bruised and battered, the bones crushed and broken. A shudder plucks my spine as my mind echoes the sound of crunching bones. His rolled-up trouser legs reveal ankles that are similarly twisted, broken and disabled. Returning my stare to meet his gaze, his mouth jolts open. His tongue is absent, cut crudely from his being.

Is this him, Oakley? The man in the Malta Times certainly, but Oakley? Whoever it is, I weakly see a victim, not a man who spat the blood of his mother.

On the floor, a metre from his feet, I notice what seems to be a passport. I pick it up and examine it. It is a UK passport in pristine condition. Taped to the cover is platinum, Visa credit card embossed with the name, Carl Hickman. An attached sticker shows the number 1005, which is my mother's birthday, the tenth of May, and also, shall I guess the PIN? I flip the passport open to the holder's page. The holder's name is, Carl Hickman and the photo is me, looking well and younger, but still, definitely me. A loose business card is printed with the words, "All yours.

Be appeased or be killed".

Is this my bounty, is this where it stops? Have I won and this is my reward?

The man, Oakley, starts nodding and shaking his head in deranged, deliberate slashes. What should I do? Is he part of the prize? Stuffing the bounty into a pocket, I get the thought to call the police. I could call the police and prove Oakley is alive. I could call the police and prove that something here is wrong, very, very wrong.

I could, and they know this. Think, Sam. They must be watching. Would they leave you here alone? No. So whoever they are, they are watching.

I step in close and put the gun to his head. I must perform as they expect me to perform. He looks at me, his eye's desperate and pleading. The shaking and nodding accelerates. I pull away and look at the phone. Already logged on to the internet, I search "malta news". A site verifies the story is true. A photo of Oakley matches the one from the paper and condemns the man in the chair. If the phone is hacked, let them see I had a reason to turn it on.

Suddenly, as if startled, I pace to the window, to the closed, full-length curtain. Using my left hand, which holds the phone, I part the curtains an inch or two and peer outside. Seeing nothing to concern me, I slip my left hand further through the gap followed by my head. The act is to look outside, but with the phone now hidden from the room, I quickly activate the video camera and start to record. Can they see this, maybe, but still, I am nothing without risk.

Stepping away from the window, I place the phone in my shirt breast pocket. As it sticks out an inch, the lens is given a clear view ahead. Reaching Oakley, I raise the gun to his face. The shaking and nodding are relentless. The gun brings him no fear. All his will, his final scrapes of energy fuel the repetitive nodding and shaking. Is it yes, or no? Is it madness or a primal scream, a plea denied the cut of words.

After a dozen or so hesitant seconds, I rush from the room and make a move for the newspapers. I pick them up and pretend to study the photo of Oakley. My real objective is to get the photo on film. Convinced it's him, I return to Oakley and ready the gun to kill.

Pulling the trigger is far from easy. I never wanted this. Would never choose this. Feel sick and angry standing here having to do this. Give me three good reasons why I should kill you. One, you deserve it. You enter the arena; you play the game. You can't change the rules when the game goes against you. Two, they expect me to. Three, I want to. Somewhere, deep down, I want to, so I do. I squeeze the trigger and end him. Another death, another murder. Another kill for me. I know this but refuse to stand and reflect any further. Instead, I turn and hurry away.

From the cold, managed chill of the house, I barge into the fierce, wild heat of the midday sun. And now, what now? Just get away. Just stay alive. A dot against nature I may be, but trapped in the crosshairs I am lame, easy prey.

Descending the hillside, I argue for both speed and restraint. In the distance, Mgarr ripples beneath a heat wave. I could walk there, find myself a room, take time out to quench my thirst, conscience and fear. I could, and should, but reaching the road, I turn and walk the other way, to Valletta. I choose pain and challenge. I choose the chance to purge the day from my being.

CHAPTER FIFTEEN

Water. No need to remind anyone that water is life. In death, most of us choose to return to the earth but me, if I can, I will be buried at sea. Returning to the earth makes no sense to me, returning to the sea, now that seems right. After all, our flesh is not earth; it is water - plus impurities.

Even this weak stream of water, falling from the shower, flushes life and vigor back into my body and soul. The water flows weakly because in Malta clean, everyday water is scarce. A laminated leaflet, placed on the closed toilet seat, asked me, the guest, to flush with care. Malta, it seems, is a resource free rock, treading saltwater in the middle of the sea.

I have taken a room in the Fortino, which was the first hotel in Valletta I came across. Physically, I am exhausted but mentally, I feel cleansed, ripe and ready for the fight. In my mind, I feel correct. My options are simple, I have only one. Continue, above and beyond Oakley. The passport, credit card and money could all help me travel the world. I could flee somewhere and anywhere, hidden but still false and tainted.

What is the credit card for, to keep me on the leech, to pay me a wage? But for what, for silence, for work?

Oakley is dead, but I still don't know why? In the eyes of many, I am still the cowardly murderer of a harmless, old lady, and this, I cannot tolerate. I don't know how, but I must dig deeper. I have evidence, enough to cause trouble and to make some demands, but not enough to clear my name. Not enough for clear and total victory.

Once clean, fed and hydrated I sleep. Seven hours later, my watch alarm wakes me. I went to bed with a gun hidden beneath the pillow; when I wake, it is gripped in my hand. Having slept fully clothed, boots and all, I rise ready to roll, a rhythm knocked off kilter by the sight of a wardrobe and sofa pushed against the door. For a moment, I feel a beat of unease until the right memory unwinds and soothes my mind.

With coffee cooling, I sit on the bed and review the video footage of Oakley. It doesn't seem real, too raw and amateur. With his death about to play, I get the urge to look away but force myself to watch. About to pull the trigger, I, him, me in the video, take a step back. Why? To stop the shower of brains, blood and flesh hitting me and my clothes. What the fuck, look at me now, on the verge of becoming a pro?

The footage clearly shows the man alive and strapped to the chair is the spit of the Oakley pictured in the newspaper. This is far from absolute proof of identity, but still, it's got to be worth something. Enough to blow smoke into the public domain.

I make a back-up copy. I take the camcorder and film the footage. Watching it play over, I see the rage in Oakley's stare. A rage I read as the rage of injustice. A man of absolute arrogance reduced to a plaything. No doubt he saw himself as something great. From the divine to a lump of meat.

What sort of man would commit the crimes he has? What would he look like? Well, if this is the template, far from average, too plain for average. Neither thin nor fat, neither pale nor tanned, neither handsome nor ugly just physically dull. Beyond the visible, I see a man too precious to be free. A man with a list of foods he fears to eat; who can't recall the last time his belly was stuffed full of food, wine or love; fearful and anxious of what he can't control, so much of life, from illness to people; groomed to be presentable, but not to get laid.

As I watch him shake and nod his head, hints of rhythm and repetition emerge. Watching over and over a pattern jumps out, both obvious and pleading. For a second, he becomes still then makes twelve shakes to the left, then one to the right, then two left, eighteen right, one left, six right, five left. The shakes become nods: one up, four down, three up, seven down, five up, two down. For a second, he pauses in stillness until shaking twelve to the left, one to the right and so on.

I rewind the footage, grab a pen from my rucksack and get ready to note the numbers down. Twelve, one, two, eighteen, one, six, five, one, four, three, seven, five, two. As numbers, they mean nothing to me, so I convert them to letters, which read LABSAFEADCHEB. Straightaway LAB SAFE jumps out, but ADCHEB? Could this mean a number? One, four, three, eight, two. Could this be the code to open the safe?

With Wi-Fi in the room, I log on to the Internet and search for answers. In an article about the crash, a local newspaper claims that Oakley was the Head of Research at the Smith Research Centre, which is located on the outskirts of Hamrun, Malta. Is this a lab, as in lab safe? I Google it, but all I learn are details of its location. I can find no company website or any other information.

Is he looking for revenge, looking for me to act on his behalf? OK, fine, but what's in it for me? Information to take me above and beyond him, to prove my innocence?

I pack my rucksack and get ready to leave. Seeing the guns, I check them for ammunition. Phillip's gun holds twenty-one rounds, the other, twenty-four.

Am I being watched? Properly paranoid, I believe the worst, so leave the hotel through a ground floor fire door, which leads to a discreet side street.

The Valletta nightlife simmers with gentle potential. All tensions burn slow and subdued. The crowds I tolerate with ease. Nighttime crowds slip past me more freely than those of the day. The night is far more forgiving and seems far more physical. There are always lies but those of the night, liberate more than those of the day.

Inside a foreign city, alone and at night, you don't as much walk as prowl. I've felt it before, that spike of adrenalin, that need to live before you die, but tonight I walk with blinkers. My only thought is to find a taxi and speed quickly away.

CHAPTER SIXTEEN

The Smith Research Centre is situated on the edge of a deserted, poorly lit industrial park that, without a retail welcome, feels cold and unwelcoming. Anonymous buildings, from small offices to medium sized factories and warehouses, all sharing the same plain, functional genes, stand muted behind wire security fences. Several lone cars, each parked on the roadside, loiter like strangers at night. The only hint of activity is the sound of heavy machinery churning in the near distance with a repetitive, grating rhythm. It is a sound that smothers, that defies a single location to emanate from all around.

At first glance, the Research Centre looks dormant for the night. It is a four-storey box, which even at night, looks bland and easily ignored: a rectangular container skinned with flat metal walls and three seamless bands of identical, blackened windows. The only feature that raises a note of interest is the brick built, windowless ground floor that seems to seal the building from the undesirable wash of the world outside. The entrance is a set of sliding doors that have been blocked for the night by an internal metal shutter. The only other entrance points are a closed external metal shutter, which is signed as the entrance to a car park, and next to it, a single, solid slab of a door that stands dead to the outside world, devoid of a handle or keyhole. An eight foot high, barbed wire crowned, perimeter fence is the first layer of defense. Fixed to its closed and locked gate are two undersized ten by ten signs. One barely announces the building to be the research centre; the other warns trespassers of security guards and guard dogs. Beyond the fence, two CCTV cameras are fixed high against each side of the building. Each camera looks down towards the centre giving a complete view of the building. Below each camera is a floodlight, which together emit enough light to make the cameras effective. I see no movement in any camera so, for now at least, I assume they are static. If so, then it seems their field of vision will be blind to the fence.

The security seems adequate and fairly discreet. Maybe there is little inside to protect, or maybe there is much to protect but little need to do so. Guard dogs and security guards, are they inside? If so, then maybe I have a way in.

Using my multi-tool, I cut a hole in the fence big enough for me to comfortably breach. Once through, I pull out Philip's gun and attach the silencer. Three shots later, and the side of the building I face falls to darkness. A quick sprint forward takes me to the door beside the car park shutter. Pressing my ear against the door, I listen and wait.

Time idles by until the faint sound of a dog's bark reaches me from beyond the door. I twist away and ready the gun, not for the guard, only the dog. The guard is no enemy of mine. Security guards are what? Men in cheap uniforms paid a click or two above the minimum wage to baby-sit inanimate objects and space. How many will take a bullet to save what means nothing to them?

Another bark, louder and more aggressive - it has the scent of battle. The door shudders against a force but remains stubbornly shut until a second force throws it open. Dim, second-hand light jumps out closely followed by an Alsatian dog, whose lust for violence is contained only by the will of its handler, a security guard. A spilt second appraisal of the guard – male, thirties, typically uniformed, athletic but a division below my weight - confirms to me my plan, a bullet to kill the dog and a punch to stun the guard. The dog duly complies, but as I raise the gun to threaten the guard his foot flies in and knocks the gun from my hand. I am instantly on the defensive fending off the professional moves of a trained martial artist. Good job I learnt the dirty way, nothing clean or controlled for me. No method to discipline or contain my rage. Physical pain served only to fuel the animal within, and the blows I now take, do nothing to tame the beast.

With my opponent down and the gun retrieved I gag his mouth and bind his hands with gaffer tape. His body is limp, his mind vacated, but still, he will live, feel and think again. From his pocket, I take a security pass. He was carrying a handheld radio, which I collect from the ground. This must mean he has backup. Who else waits inside? A voice speaks over the radio - male and English:

'Carl, speak to me!'

Mindful of CCTV inside the building, I approach the door, which remains wide open, with caution. The radio voice returns with urgency:

'Carl!...Carl! Hans, go check, Carl!'

'Give me a minute,' another voice, male and German.

'For fuck's sake! Do it now!'

'One minute!'

'Now!'

'I'm takin' a shit!'

'For fuck's sake!'

Reaching the door, I peer inside and see the ground floor of an underground car park. A CCTV camera covers the entire space. Opposite me, I see a door. A sign fixed to it tells me it leads to an elevator and stairwell. The radio voice loses patience,

'Hans, I'm going. You come back here, now!'

Here? The control room? I take the risk that the CCTV will be, briefly, unmanned. I run towards the door. Once through, I take the stairs. Now to find Oakley's office and look for the safe. Knowing time is against me, I sprint up towards the top floor, where I hope vanity will insist the boss reside.

The stairwell is cold, clean and efficient, a place where only the desperate would linger. Nothing distracts from its purpose. Heavy, solid doors deny a glimpse of what floors two and three contain. The only signs are floor numbers. No other information is shared. Reaching floor four, I slowly peel back the door to reveal a long, well-lighted corridor. I slip inside and hurry along.

The corridor shares the stairwell's hostility and houses ten doors, five on either side. Each door is labelled 4a, 4b and so on. No windows, in the doors or walls, offer a view of what exists on the other side. Passing door 4e curiosity takes the better of me, and I boot the door open. Inside I find a large room with bare white walls, floor and ceiling. In the air, a chill and hum hang. Arranged in the centre of the floor is a twelve by twelve grid of large computers units. Each one is identical - matt black in colour, rectangular in shape and three feet tall. They stand like monoliths, inanimate but strangely powerful, as if knowing - learning. A CCTV camera records every beat of stillness.

I pull myself a way and continue ahead. At the end of the corridor, a right turn leads to another door, one signed Oakley Miles Robertson. It is locked, so I kick it open. Inside cold, scientific efficiency is replaced with plush, corporate extravagance. It is a space more akin to high-end finance then the daily toil of scientific research. Employing the most obvious choice first, I pull a large digital photo frame, showing an image of the 'The Scream', from a wall. No safe is hidden beneath it. I move to his desk, a fortress of dark, shining wood, and open all the draws. The largest opens on a vertical hinge and reveals a safe hidden within. An electronic keypad takes the code, and the door clicks open. I reach inside and remove a single, lone item, a sealed, stiff-backed, A4 vanilla envelope. On the front is a hand written Malta address, addressed to a person called Rosemary Cassavetes. Over the radio, the voice of Han:

'I'm back. Steve, where are you?'

I rip open the envelope and pull out the contents, a printed report of fifty or so pages. The front page reads:

"Desalination Through The Use Of The Miles-Robertson Filter. An organic nanotech filter for removing salt content from seawater. Summary of key benefits: cheap, low energy way of producing substantial amounts of clean drinking water from seawater. Inventor of The Miles-Robertson filter Oakley Miles Robertson. Report author, Oakley Miles Robertson."

Is this is? Is this what he wants me to find? Why? Is this all it is?

Over the radio, Steve,

'We have a problem. Radio compromised.'

Confused, and somehow angered with a strange feeling of betrayal, I stuff the report into my rucksack then focus on my escape. It is me against them, me against the building.

Back in the corridor, running along, gun primed and tightly held. I must be outnumbered, two to one at least. Is my advantage held in my hand, or will they now level the field? I know I can't pause; I know I can't hide. Time can only move the odds against me. I enter the stairwell. The stairs or the lift? I press the button and make my call. The doors start to open. I make ready the gun, but the curtains reveal an empty stage. A look inside sparks an idea. I jump towards the roof and punch open a service door. A shaft is exposed; a space to hide. I send the lift to the car park then haul myself up and out, into darkness I rise. As the lift begins to sink, I anchor my focus to the square of light beneath me. Dim lines of light check me past the doors on floors three and two. The lift stops sharply. My view of the door is blocked, but I hear and feel it open. I stand in darkness, looking at the light below, a finger poised to sanction another. The stage, however, remains empty. As the doors begin to close, I jump down and out.

Ahead into the stairwell and all is clear. Now a race to the door which leads to the car park. Five metres away and I finish second. The door flies open, and in lunges a security guard. Seeing my advantage, he instantly yields. His body tenses and rebounds to a stop, stunned by a brief taste of mortality.

'Fuck you!' he screams. He's English; he's Steve.

My inaction frees him; he begins to move delicately around me. Keeping the gun aimed at his head, I begin to move towards the door. He watches me with an angry, disappointed stare. Not enough sport at the best of times, and tonight he's missed the fight. Reaching the door, I take it with a fresh burst of speed.

Now back in the car park, running towards the door that was dead to the outside world. It is closed, fully and completely shut. Reaching it, I push it, shoulder it then kick it. Ever violent, but all I need is a key. I glance behind; Steve watches me. He grins, excitement shifts disappointment. Desperate, I fire five rounds into the steel skinned door and lock. The bullets are absorbed; the door remains defiant. Steve, ever eager, is flipping his stare between the stairwell and me. On the wall, I see a small, grey metal box with a closed, possibly locked door. Stepping towards it, I fire a round into its lock. The door flies open. Inside I see a control panel. A quick inspection reveals a button labeled Open, which I press and hold. The metal shutter rumbles into life. A look towards the stairwell reveals Steve ducking behind the door. The shutter begins to rise. Looking back towards the stairwell, the door opens and in probes the barrel of a shotgun. A bullet from my gun snaps it back. I lash out with two more bullets and disable the CCTV camera glaring down at me. The shutter climbs a foot high. I step away, releasing the button, but the shutter continues to rise. Diving to the ground, I smash a bullet into the control panel. The shutter stops, instantly. Hitting the ground, I roll outside.

Back on my feet, a sprint to the fence. Once through and clear, I simply run, fast and free. Reaching a lone parked car I make my move. I try the door handle, and the door just opens. I climb inside and try my luck, I pull the sun visor down where, wonder-of-wonders, I find the key. Pulling away, the rear view mirror shows a deserted scene. Am I too far ahead to see clearly, or have they paused, making plans for another time?

Driving, to where, I question my actions. How does this paper advantage me? How can I use it to prove my innocence? What good is it to me? I can do with it, what? Publish it? Let Oakley take the credit? Was this is final act of arrogance?

What else can it tell me? Why was the envelope addressed? He was posting it, why? Back-up? Just in case, of what? Was there more, more discoveries and innovations? Make a hard copy and post them somewhere safe, just in case?

The Miles-Robertson filter, of course, named after him. Miles Robertson, Colonel Miles Robertson. The story at the end of the novel, Bunker14382 - the numbers, the code to open the safe. The web page, on her laptop the night I broke in, it showed a science paper, his science paper. Password protected. He gave her access to read his work, 'educate yourself', and then she wrote the story, Bunker14382. I need Wi-Fi.

I race back to Valletta; I must get back to the hotel. A risk, I know, but one I must take.

CHAPTER SEVENTEEN

Inside my hotel room, connected to the Internet. From the email, I click the link to open the page. The password box demands compliance. I enter "bunker14382" then click enter. The page hangs for a second then continues to load. I am accepted as valid. The page design is basic, a white page showing nothing more than a row of folder icons. The names of the icons include Work, Messages, People, Research, Fucking, and Mother. Seeing the Mother icon, I open it up. A page loads which contains a single video icon named, Birthday. I select the icon, click and play. A video player opens, and a video begins to play. It shows Oakley and his mother in split screen. Both are filmed at computers by webcams. The mother is clearly at home, sitting at her desk in a brightly lit room. Oakley's surroundings are lost to darkness. His face is illuminated with lighting that looks staged and designed to flatter with a soft, warm glow. He speaks, and his head remains perfectly still, knowingly stuck in the plane of good lighting.

'My, my, mother.'

'Oakley.'

'Can you see me?'

'Yes.'

'So here we are. Once again, visible…You've read the papers.'

'I have. Has anyone else?'

'Of course,' he says, amused as if the question was stupid.

'Who?'

'People.'

'Who exactly?'

'People.'

'Who?'

'All the right people. The privileged. Just like you tonight.'

'Look at you. I haven't seen you for so many years.'

'Have you been counting? I didn't bother. But look at me, haven't I prospered.'

'Prospered, but into what?'

'Into me! Into the right man for me! And you, published your first novel yet?'

'No, but thank you, you're quite the inspiration.'

'Oh, if only you had the mind to imagine. But anyway, tell me, my work, have I impressed you?'

'Do you need to?'

'Of course. I am human, after all. Let me crave recognition with the rest of them.'

'Then why haven't you published?'

'Guess. Imagine.'

'Profit'

'Nothing so crude.'

'Then what?'

'Life, mother! Existence, for all those who matter!'

'We all matter!'

'Do we? How quaint.'

'We do!'

'No, we don't. A simple truth, but one so many fear to acknowledge.'

'But not you, my son?'

'Your son is a scientist, and as a scientist, he welcomes truth, truth and observation, and believe me, there is nothing your son fears to observe, or to know.'

'And the truth is yours to decide?'

'To discover and accept.'

'If what I've read is true you could save the lives of so many people. Your work, it could offer hope to so many.'

'Yes, it could. The work I do, and the work of others. But hope to who exactly, to the desperate? It's always the desperate! You should be sick of the desperate! It's always the desperate who need to be saved! However much we endeavor, however much we invest they never seemed to be cured!'

'Hope to us all!'

He laughs, contemptuously. Then speaks,

'Us all? Us? We, are all one? In the distance maybe. In fact way back, way back! But now, no! And not going forward either!'

'Who do you work for? For whose benefit?'

'For the greater good. For the bigger picture.'

'And your company? Your organization? Your institute?'

'Nameless.'

'Nameless?

'How can you know what you can never understand?'

'Then your objective?'

'To offer hope. Hope for the world, and for all those who remain. Hope, which will soon be released. Be grateful you'll miss it.'

'Who is it you work for?!'

'The future of man.'

'Oh for Christ's sake! Is this act for my benefit? To make me swoon at your importance. To make me believe you're as important as you think you are?'

He laughs, arrogant, with a sense of victory, then continues,

'Do you remember me as a child, mother? Do you? Do you remember me, your child? Do you remember how my favorite television was always natural history? How I would sit and watch hours and hours, fixed and fascinated? Do you remember telling me I watched too much, that I should go outside and play? I do. I remember all these things. I remember how, even then, you would annoy and frustrate me. I remember me, sitting happy and contented, watching and learning, and you hovering, pest-like, waiting to censor, remote control in hand. I remember you, pouncing as soon as any violence, or sex, was shown. You, censoring what I could watch. You, denying me truth. It's why I hated history at school. It bored me. It bored me because they didn't teach the sex or the violence. Now, of course, history isn't all sex and violence but still, give me the facts! Give me the truth!'

'The truth? And what is your truth, here and now? Who are you?'

'I read an interview with David Attenborough. He recalled a letter he received from a woman, a plainly stupid woman, who after watching one of his programmes, one that documented a pride of lions, felt compelled to write and express her anger, and disgust, at the violent and murderous lions. Her solution, stop wasting money on making such television programmes and instead use the money saved to train the lions to stop killing animals. Can you imagine? I can still taste the hate I felt for her. Let us civilize nature and history. Let us deny the truth of whom and what we are.'

'We're not animals.'

'No, of course not. We are moral.'

'We? You could offer so much hope?'

'If it is immoral to let a child be raised in poverty, then isn't it also immoral to give birth to that child in the first place? The world has enough cheap labour, enough commitments to feed and save. Do the math, mother, because we won't be moving to Mars any time soon.'

'Meaning?'

'To ease the load on our beautiful earth. That, is a moral crusade worth fighting for! What joy for the human race if we could fly away to another earth, but no, we cannot. We are fixed, penned in, and like any herd, it must be managed.'

'I really don't know you. I have no instinct for you.'

'Instinct, how pathetic. You can't calculate me! Why? Because you don't know me. You don't have sufficient information on whom or what I am.'

'No, no I don't.'

'Christ, how you bore me. I had removed you from the equation, but you had to come looking. Now, I cannot, I will not tolerate your presence. You're a nuisance, an agitation. I move in far greater circles than you could ever hope to cope with. The power I can exercise; the power I feel obliged to test, is nothing you could ever comprehend. So, goodbye, mother. You have had you time, and now, I return you to nothing.'

A human figure steps into shot behind her. He, of course a he, is wearing a dark coloured protective overall suit. As he walks towards her, his face remains off-camera. Oakley watches with a calm, intrigued stare. The mother turns with a jolt of surprise. The figure casually jabs her in the face with a gloved left-fist. Her body folds. He yanks her up by pulling her hair, then contains her struggle with a smothering left arm wrapped around her face and head. Bending down to eyeball the web cam, the figure becomes Phillip. His right-hand brings a meat tenderizer to his forehead, and with it, he offers Oakley a lazy salute. Oakley offers no reply. Phillip drags the mother away. The struggle she offers is feeble, barely whispering defiance. Oakley continues to watch. Even with his mother dragged from the room and out of shot, he continues to silently stare. After ten or so seconds, the video ends, and the clip turns black.

Proof! I have my proof! I have my innocence to touch and share!

With a panicked rush, I try and save the video to disk but the video player has no toolbar, no menu to click and save. The panic intensifies as I scramble to grab the camcorder from my rucksack. I will film the video, film it and flee. Film it and shout to the world, I did not kill her and here is the proof!

I sit filming and watching. Two people are drawn back into life. A mother and her son, together without touching. What difference between them is there really to know?

I wanted to understand, I wanted to know why and now I have his answer. He killed her because she was a nuisance, a simple agitation. What path does a man have to travel to allow him so slight an excuse? Who was he? Who were his people? He suppressed his work, as did others, work that could save the lives of people, but why? To save this beautiful earth? But from what? People, too many people? The earth does carry a heavy weight. We have trapped it, caged it and now we bleed it to feast on it. Too many people, god, how I know. I have felt crushed in the flow, but we the people are the most precious resource - assholes, beggars, thieves, the gutless and soulless, we are all still the people. What is the earth without us? How beautiful can it really be?

To deny the world technology that could save lives? I don't see why. To let people die? For pleasure? For belief? His work, and the work of others. How many? To what extent and scale? He and his colleagues have the means to save lives but choose purposefully not to do so. So, every day they kill, every day they murder. No news to me, but still, why?

His stare, all the sickness of man I can see in his stare. Watching him watch his mother being dragged away I actually feel fear. Fear for what is out there. Fear for what it is possible to be.

The clip, with a second or two to play, suddenly freezes. I try to move the cursor over the play button, but it too has frozen. The sound of the hard drive whirring frantically away tells me some process continues to run. I randomly hit a dozen or so keys, but none causes any action. Have they hacked the laptop? Are they destroying the hard drive? Let them! The proof is taped; the proof is mine!

They know my location. I must think this way; I must think the worst. I must think that Malta is too small to resist them, that my instinct for England is right.

I grab my belongings and get ready to flee. But the people, the assholes, beggars and thieves, the good, the bad, the desperate. How many do I walk away from? What hope do I leave uncovered? The science paper, enveloped and addressed, ready to post, but why? For backup, to prove ownership and a date of completion? Print off a copy and post it to someone who knows nothing, just the order to store it, to keep it safe until, well, until now. Rosemary Cassavetes, Rosemary was the name on the post-it note. So, his cleaner or housekeeper maybe? Someone under his control, someone out of the loop. Who would think a cleaner has anything to hide? And if she does, what hope could be mine to uncover?

Complete, I leave.

The corridor outside my room is deserted. Hurrying myself along, I rush towards the elevator. As I reach it, the door jumps open. Inside is planted a thick-set man in his mid to late thirties. Dressed as a member of hotel staff, in a suit that looks a size too small, he stands rigidly as if guarding his own importance. His blank, unfriendly stare clocks me for a second then leaves to look at nothing. The sparkle of a diamond studded earring, and the glint of a heavy gold bracelet seal his fate. I launch an untamed punch towards his face. It connects and he drops unconscious to the floor. As the door closes, I search his pockets. The gun I expect to find is missing. His only weapon is the proverbial pen.

The elevator begins to descend, next stop reception. I fix my stare forward, look beyond all that blocks my way. The elevator slows to a stop. The door opens, and I pounce, out through a blur of people, across reception, to the exit and out. Running, sprinting. No doubt people look and stare, but I pay them no attention and offer no reply .My legs speed me back to the car, which in turn speeds me back to Mgarr.

CHAPTER EIGHTEEN

Mgarr. I have arrived quietly and alone. Its narrow, pre-car streets harass my search but eventually, and with luck, I find the address I'm looking for - a ground floor apartment in a three storey block. And now, what now? Knock the door and what? Force? Explain? Charm? At this hour, eleven at night? The curtains are drawn, and a gentle light contained within. I could wait then break in, but if she woke, what would I do to shut her up? Is she alone? Could she be, in a street as densely packed as this? This isn't right. Not now. I start the engine and pull away.

Oakley's house. Black without light. I park, tuck the car into a field then walk up the lane to the house. Reaching the grounds, I stand and listen. Silence, more than before, not even the sound of falling water. With gun in hand, I walk to the door. Finding it locked, I ring the bell for a good twenty seconds. No sound or movement answers back, so I kick the door open and let myself in.

I stand, listening. Again silence. The darkness washed by the light from my torch. No alarms have sounded, not here, not to scare, but maybe elsewhere to warn and inform. My plan is simple, look for his phone. I find it, one handset at least, neatly placed on a bare kitchen table. Scrolling through the menu, I find the phonebook and then what I came for, two numbers assigned to Rosemary, her home and mobile numbers.

Does the phone send and receive text messages? It does. I call Rosemary's mobile. After a dozen rings, the call is answered,

'Hello,' a female voice, soft and nervous, but then her phone is telling her a ghost is calling.

I cancel the call. Then quickly write and send her a text message, which reads:

"The envelopes. I need them, tonight. By Oakley's request."

Less than a minute later, I receive a reply.

"When? Where?"

I reply.

"Your house. 10 minutes?"

"Yes"

"I'm coming."

Could the house offer me anything more? Possibly. Time though dictates my action. Back to the car and then, again, to Mgarr.

I park opposite her apartment. Nothing seems to have changed. Other than a group of male youths hanging out on parked mopeds, the streets are empty.

Stepping out of the car, the sound of a helicopter, distant but nearing, disturbs the sleepy peace. Holding the envelope from the safe, and displaying it as some sort of ID, I quickly approach the apartment. Reaching the door, I gently knock. It opens immediately, shy and mistrusting. Hunched behind the dark, narrow opening I glimpse an elderly woman who I assume must be Rosemary. Without looking at me, she passes a canvass holdall through the gap and drops it on the ground.

'Go, quickly. People are watching,' she says, hushed and impatient.

She pulls the door firmly shut. I take the bag, which is heavier than I expect, and return to the car. People, who? Neighbours?

Inside the car, I put the envelope back in the rucksack then unzip the holdall to check inside. There are at least twenty, well-packed, A4 envelopes, sealed and addressed. Not wishing to linger I start the car and pull away.

Once clear of the town, I accelerate hard into the countryside. As far as I can tell I am all alone. Nobody is watching or following, at least not from the road.

Slowing the car, I give in to curiosity. I take an envelope from the holdall, rip it open and pull out the paper. The front page is blank. Page two and three, blank. Flipping through, every page is blank. This means?

I slam on the brakes, grab the rucksack then, with the speed dipping to forty, open the door and throw myself out. I hit the road hard, with the rucksack cradled protectively between my chest and my forearms. Crunched in the fetal position, instinct gives me the sense to roll my body over the scraping road. A flash of light explodes into my eyes; a shockwave smashes through me and a sound wave stabs at my ears. A dry stone wall stops me dead. Breath and energy collapse from within me. I hear shrapnel hitting the ground around me, but I have no movement to protect me. The car, raging with fire and spinning like a demented firework, drags to a halt in the middle of the road. A flashing light in the sky, the helicopter, catches my eye. Is it them, here to watch? Well, let them see me dead. I toss the rucksack over the wall, as gently as I can, then haul my leaden body towards the burning car. If they are watching, they must use thermal imaging cameras. If so, let me vanish into the heat print of the car. I crawl through the dense, hot air as close as I can then a metre more. Turning my back to take the lashings of heat, I lay on the rapidly warming asphalt. My lungs, spared the fumes, which rise vertically into a windless sky, burn with every timid breath I take. The helicopter continues to hover. My hair and clothes, full with heat, begin to burn and singe. Several minutes pass until I hear the sound of a siren approaching. Finally, the helicopter speeds away.

I scramble to the side of the road and leap over the dry stone wall. In the field, I recover the rucksack. A flashing blue beacon rapidly nears. I turn and run. My injuries queue to take a scream. Having cleared fifty plus metres, I hurdle the wall and take to the road.

Am I dead? Do they celebrate my death, the killing of a problem?

With a good mile already banked, the whining sound of a moped engine catches me from behind. I turn and look, a single headlight jostles my way. As it reaches me, it slows. Two male youths, the rider and passenger, are amused at my current situation. They pull up beside me and mouth some words of discouragement. It takes no thought at all. I lash out and knock them from their ride. With the moped floundering, I free it from the ground and take it as my ride.

Am I invisible? How long before they know? If they celebrate my death, then I have time. Time to disappear or time to move closer?

Make a decision then pursue it without fear. Once again, I hear my mother's voice. Once again, I see her, full of fear. Full of fear but never, not once, did she cower. Never broken. Let all fear in. Take it. Absorbed it. Accept all consequence.

The Research Centre, what else is in there? What else can I take and learn? Would they expect me to return? Would they expect me to never run away?

CHAPTER NINETEEN

The Hamrun Industrial Park, no change here, still the only sign of life is the machine driven hum. Having parked the moped, I approach the Research Centre on foot. From a distance, all appears peaceful. As I close-in, the peace is confirmed. For now they tolerate the hole in the fence and the shot-up CCTV. The dog and the guard, however, are gone. The car park shutter remains as I left it, raised just enough to let me squeeze under. Through the gap, a wall of weak, hazy light spills out.

With gun in hand, I shuffle through the hole in the fence. Once through, I move quickly to the side of the shutter, where I pause, straining to sense any movement from within. With nothing detected, I crouch down and peer inside. No threat leaps out, no menace glares. The CCTV camera remains disabled. I take to the ground and push myself under the shutter, it ripples with clangs and bangs.

Back on my feet, I freeze in a shooting position, poised ready to fire on any sign of life. Without a target or a sound to explore, I move towards the stairwell door. As I reach it, a sound jumps from beyond it, the solid thud of a heavy door closing. I rebound to the side of the door, gun aimed and ready. The door is pushed open and out slips a guard, Hans? Do I shoot to kill, to maim or tame? Before I can answer, I lunge forward and smash the gun handle into the side of his neck. A punch, or two, later and the final flashes of his consciousness have been stubbed-out. He hits the ground, a dummy for me to tie and gag.

I reach the stairwell door. With gun probing, I tease the door open. Alone, I step inside, pause and listen. To the stairwell, the lift or the door ahead?

Where is the other guard? Where does he sit and watch? I move to the door ahead, and with the security pass I took from Carl, unlock it. No teasing, no probing, I barge inside and take the space, bold and blatant, fearless with nothing to hide. Steel steps take me down into a white, harshly lit corridor. A CCTV camera films my every move. As I rush towards an opened door, the voice of Steve booms my way.

'Hans, he's fractured...'

Steve lumbers out from behind the door and into a savage fist. Am I now alone, silent and invisible? Invisible and omnipresent, for inside the room, a wall of monitors allows complete and total vision. The centre is mine to know, but all I can see, the only focus I can pull is on a face, a close-up of a man, whose face is still, perfectly still, except for a stare that barely contains a mass of raging, menaced thoughts. His black skin is primed with a glutinous sweat and torn with sores, those beacons spewing pain. This is the photo on the South African's phone, live but dying, a different man but the same disease.

For relief, I look away and find a wider view. On a monitor below I see a laboratory, a standard science lab, standard but for three black men all imprisoned in three glass cages. They are all naked, slumped, lifeless, on the floor in bare, glass cells.

I look at Steve, who has started to regain consciousness. Taking the gaffer tape, I bind his hands behind his back. As he starts to recognise me, and the situation he is in, I thrust the barrel of the gun deep into his mouth. His stare offers defiance, but not enough to mask his fear. Convinced he doesn't underestimate my will, I step back, and with a flick of the gun, beckon him to stand. He complies and rises effortlessly to his feet. Once up, I grab him from behind, and with an explosive burst of aggression, power him into the room where I smash his face hard into the monitor, into the man and his disease. As I twist his face into the screen, his pained and angered voice erupts,

'What?!...Show you?!'

I throw him out of the room. Gun aimed and ready to kill. Catching his stare, I nod my head.

'You're here for them? For fuck's sake. What the fuck is this to you?'

I gesture with the gun for him to walk, which he does without protest.

'You think this can end with you winning? Who the fuck are you anyway? Who the fuck do you think you are!'

We pass a door labelled, "Maintenance" then reach another, labelled B1. He stops.

'There. And that's all you'll get from me, motherfucker!'

I push him away then unlock the door with the security pass. Pulling the door open, I gesture for him to enter. He complies, forcing out a laugh as he passes me.

'You good for this?'

I follow him in and, seeing the lab, ram a full-strength punch into his kidneys. As he collapses to the floor, I, too, feel the wind punched out of me. Three men in three glass cages, lab rats, vulnerable and abused. The basic rules of civilization do not, here, apply. I approach one of the men, his stomach pumps with short, rapid breaths. The sores cover his starved, desperate body. He makes no movement to look at me. Flies, mosquitoes, I don't know, swarm inside the cage. Is he their feast? Has he been thrown to them, as meat? I rush to the guard, still wounded on the floor, stamp my foot into his throat and aim the gun at his face. He knows what I want, I want answers. Choking, he spits them out.

'Fuck you! Nothing more from me, motherfucker!! This ain't no nine to five! I want this!! I want this!! Do it!! Fuckin' do it!'

I pull the trigger, in my head I see me pull the trigger but, bang, a fist pounds against a glass cell. I turn. The African Man is looking at me, recognising my presence. I step toward the cell. He wants to speak. I crouch down, face-to-face with him. His deep, heavy African accent slithers through the glass.

'Burn us…Kill it…Burn us.'

The cell door has a pull mechanism. I move to grab it.

'No!' he pleads. I stop.

'Disease. Into mosquito, into us, and into Africa! Burn it! Burn it! We are dead. There is no cure!'

Couldn't I just call the police? What doubt can there be? I move to the guard and search his pockets.

'Burn it! Ha! Fuckin' African's! Too much voodoo. It's the primitive mind!'

I pull a mobile phone from his pocket.

'Won't work, no signal. Not here. Go upstairs. Call the police? No. C'mon. Don't destroy this! Join us!'

Call the police? Not now. Not now you want me to.

And now? What now? A disease, new or modified? Man-made by them? Into Africa and into man. But why? Has the world enough cheap labour? To slash and burn, to destroy and create, to save this beautiful earth?

Think. Act. Film the evidence. Andrew's phone, could it be traced without a signal? Reaching for it, I remember Henry's phone. Could it film what I see? Could it offer me clues? I slip off my rucksack and pull out the phone. As I turn it on, I move back to the African. Can I save him? If I free him will I also free the disease? He speaks, running on empty. His need to convince me is all that fuels him.

'Burn it! Everything! Everything! Destroy it!' he demands.

He must tell me, Steve, he must tell me! As I turn to face him, an alarm starts to buzz, sharp and penetrating. He has risen from the floor. To mock me, he repeats the action I missed, he throws a kick at a wall mounted alarm. I rush to him, the gun aimed at his face.

'You think I give a fuck. You think that's ugly to me? Well wrong. It's beautiful!!'

Then suffer for it. I pound punches and kicks into his body and face. As he falls to the floor, I aim a kick at his left knee. The kick connects and snaps the joint in two. His agony is his anchor and pins him to the floor.

The alarm looks like a standard fire alarm, but who I wonder is now speeding this way? Too much knowledge for me to control. I wanted to take some for the good of whomever, but now? Now, this place must burn. I hunt for and find two gas taps. Leaving them off, I run towards the door. About to exit, I remember Henry's phone. If the signal returns, then so be it.

Into the corridor. Hunting fuel on every floor; gas taps turned on, flammable liquids smashed and released, pilot lights lit. No humans or animals found, although my search is incomplete. I can only destroy, I cannot save. As I go, I check the phone for clues and information. A call was made to Spitz, to a landline number in London. Could this give me his address? The only text is from someone named Fox, which reads:

"Is your GOD capable of this? Is HE the one to save us? You may have found HIM but pray you haven't lost us."

Attached is a video file, which I play and watch. A computer generated animation shows a volcanic island, alone in the middle of an ocean. An explosion, not an eruption but an explosion running the length of the island causes half the island to crash into the ocean. The displaced water rises up and forms a tsunami that speeds away towards the horizon. The shot dissolves into a bird's eye view of the ocean. The tsunami is tracked as it races towards the African coastline. Another dissolve, the tsunami reaches land. Desperation and devastation as people, animals and buildings are all consumed by the wave.

Is this a threat, a plan, an ambition? I, myself, am feeling drowned. In the Maintenance Room, I turn off the water supply and pull leads from an emergency generator.

Back to the lab. I have returned with two, large gas bottles. Placing them next to Steve, I open the values and let gas spew into the air. No mask hides his fear.

'You want me to talk? I don't know anythin'. Nothin' more than this!'

I ignore him, completely blank him. I rush to the gas taps, turn one on to a gentle flow then, using my cigarette lighter, ignite the gas to create a pilot light - a whisper waiting to roar.

With the Henry's phone, I film more evidence. Not of my innocence, but of the crimes committed around me. The conscious African watches me. He is calm but has no strength to speak. I pause, watching him, flicking my stare between him on the screen and him for real. Another life about to end, another story about to finish.

And now, what now, do I let them burn? Do I turn and run? Do I flee into a darkness where this death I will never be see for real? A bullet would be easier for them, but for me? Can I risk contact with the disease? Can I risk a spark from the gun? Can I add more kills to my name?

I turn and move to leave. The guard screams a will to confess, adding,

'We're getting paid. We deport 'em, tonight! This is for us, but we deport 'em. By boat, from Valletta, tonight! You can make it. You can make it! The Fallen Fresco. Check the times! You can make it!!'

I continue on my way, rushing into the corridor until something pulls me back. Whipping out my cigarette lighter, I spark a flame then throw it into the lab straight at Steve. A fireball ignites around him - this man, this

Guy, this fuel for empty flames. With room to step around the fire, and Steve's fading scream, I take my position, smash each cage with a bullet then beat the disease to its goal.

With a second to spare, I twist free of an explosion. Into the corridor I flee. A quick look through my all seeing eye reveals a blitzkrieg of fire and explosion.

In the car park, Hans remains disabled. I pass him without thought or concern.

Out into the night, where sirens and fire give life to the stagnant streets. I clear the fence then sprint away, away from the sirens and the moped, away from a newly parked car, and away from an inferno that destroys as it saves.

Running directionless, swirling, sucked towards the centre. I take a dozen turns but remain trapped in the Industrial Park. The sirens fall silent. A helicopter's warning light flashes in the sky, like a missile on a radar screen seconds from a target.

I take another turn and see another car, parked twenty metres ahead. Its shape and dark colour match that of the newly parked car. Suspicion fails to slow me. I have no time to be nervous, or to move with subtle care.

With gun in hand, I reach the car. It is empty, and the bonnet is hot. I try the driver's door; it opens. How and why? Is this for me, a special delivery for me? I slip inside. No key in the ignition, but the sun visor? Yes, a key. I take it and stab it into the ignition. About to turn it, I stop. Make a decision. Do they need to blow me up? Am I that slippery, that dangerous? Fuckin' shoot me! It's easier, easier to clean-up the mess. I turn the key, and the engine starts.

I have speed. Coincidence or conspiracy? Whatever, it's mine, and I'll take it.

I want to show control. I want to drive like I have nothing to hide, but I drive like a man set loose from a deranged, screaming spirit, with everything to hide but no place to dump it.

Finding the edge of the Industrial Park, I take a road to Valletta. The road is mine and mine alone. Solitude, again, is my victory.

Reaching Valletta, I park the car. A quick look outside confirms my solitude. Two helicopters hang in the sky but are too distant to concern me. Back inside the car, I take Steve's phone and connect to the Internet. With Spitz's number still fresh in my mind, I give it to Google and click for results. A link takes me to a website for a company called Deep Blue Solutions. The number relates to their London office. The home page describes them as a private security firm and claims that they:

"provide strategic support to governments and the commercial sector in the specialist niche of security and intelligence related services with particular emphasis upon designing and implementing solutions related to international terrorism, security force capability and complex geopolitical issues."

Meaning what? They'll fight for you, or for your money at least. With their website otherwise sterile, I Google the company name and find a newspaper article titled "The Fat Cats of War." It labels them a private military company and reports that two of their employees, who in 2008 were working as private security guards in Iraq, were arrested and charged with the murder of sixteen civilian people including women and children. A week before their trial came to court the men escaped from prison and were never seen again. The article goes on to report that the company has worked in Afghanistan and Iraq under contract from the US military. It is also believed that they have considerable connections in Africa and are known to have provided the dictatorship in Equatorial Guinea security and military support. Claims have also been made that they have trained numerous rebel and gorilla groups throughout the African continent, mainly those fighting for control of precious natural resources. The founder, John Spitz is an American, ex-special forces and connected in Washington. A photo of him shows a business suited skinhead sitting at a plush, office desk. A faint, unsatisfied smile is forced for the camera. His posture is perfect, and his stare is charmless, open only for business. The article states his age is forty-eight, but here he looks younger with an upper torso that is broad and muscular.

Is this my man? Is this the man with whom it could end?

"We are one but not the same."

The same as whom, the brains and the money? Because they are what, the muscle? They work together, but for what? For tonight? Into Africa and into man? Unwanted immigrants arrive in Malta. Some get returned with immediate effect, but others, from so-called unsafe countries, can't be booted right around. The law and lawyers see to that. The solution, slip beneath the law. A solution Spitz and his people use to their own advantage, to colour a piece of the bigger picture, which is what? To spread disease, to suppress scientific innovation, to instigate mass murder! To fuck with me, to draw me down, to turn me into a man who can kill on demand? I was a free man, never afraid to be still, but now, here I am forever rooted in frenzy. To the harbour. To the ship. To what, to kill some more?

CHAPTER TWENTY

I drive as close as I can get. Valletta rests on a hill. Once free of the car I run the final distance up towards the high ground. Ancient, old world fortifications peel away and expose a clear, panoramic view of the harbour. I stand, trespassing on a tourist perch, one adorned with flower beds, benches and canon. Before me, the harbour steals the horizon. Darkness blurs the finer details, although clusters of artificial light expose enough to give me options. A marina, a container port, a cruise ship terminal and a quayside can all be detected. Instinct draws me towards the quayside, where a single ship is berthed. The illuminated bridge, along with several spotlights fixed to the ship, emboss the surrounding darkness with animated human figures. I draw my binoculars and scour the ship for a name, but the lack of light keeps me blind.

Could the Fallen Fresco be a yacht, a container ship or a cruise liner? No. A bold guess, I know, but still, give me instinct over ignorance, and time, what time is there left?

I make safe the video memory card; it is more precious than me. Together with the passport, credit cards, Andrew's and Henry's phones and the remaining cash, I seal it in a plastic bag then bind it with lashings of gaffer tape.

Kneeling beside a flowerbed I use my hands to burrow into the earth. I then bury and hide my innocence. After committing the location to memory, I discard the now useless camcorder then stand and make my move.

Down to the quayside. A steep flight of ancient stone steps offers passage to yet another man, armed and hunting blood. Who were the Knights who fought for Malta? What was their cause? Was it better than mine? Did they, too, plead the good of man?

On the quayside all is quiet, no man-made noise just the lazy breath of a dozing sea and the whispered resistance of a casual breeze. The ship doesn't fail the mood. The embossed human figures have melted away. A lone man, dispatched to smoke a cigarette, and cloaked in a military-style overcoat, stands on the quayside next to a gangway that connects to the ship to land. My presence is urgently sensed then casually ignored. The ship is large, a good seventy metres in length. Nearing the bow, I read its name, The Fallen Fresco. As I approach the man, he turns his back to me and slowly ambles away, waiting for me to pass. I make no apologies, draw the gun from a pocket and, with a point blank accuracy, aim, fire and kill. The silencer keeps the mood calm and still. Catching the man's body as it slumps to the ground, I carry it to the edge of the quay and quietly feed it the sea.

To board the ship, I have a simple choice, walk the gangway or climb a mooring rope, I choose to climb. Twenty metres of rope is no easy haul, especially with rope too thick to wrap a good grip around. As the climb nears completion, cramp tears into my hands, and I barely manage to pull myself up and over the railing.

Without thought to pause and recover my hands, I snatch a gun from a pocket then move forwards over a small area of deck at the stern of the ship. Reaching the superstructure, I find a door. The handle yields to an angry force. As the door creaks open, a tunnel of darkness appears within. I duck inside and ease the door shut.

Touch tells of a low, narrow space contained by cold steal walls. Three steps forward and a dead-end is reached. Following the raised edge of what I hope is a door I feel for, and find, a handle. Pushing it down, the door is released, as is a loud clunking noise, which persists in an echo. I freeze, waiting for silence. With the echo dead, I slowly push the door open. Harsh, white light rushes in and rips sight back into my eyes. Another short corridor stands before me, a crossroads with the choice of another closed door, or a hatch in the floor that leads to a ladder and the deck below. A devil's choice, so I choose to go down.

The ladder takes me to a long, deserted corridor. Two flickering fluorescent bulbs provide insufficient light. Several doors line the walls, and a hatch in the floor leads to a second deck below. If I have a plan it is to find the cheap space, space drenched with the roar of the engine and used for the cheapest of cargos. So again the ship sucks me down.

I descend the ladder with slow, forensic care. Into the guts of the ship. Pipes, tubes and wiring clog another corridor, another space devoid of people where the shadows have flushed the light.

In the air, the muffled beginnings of a song skim over silence - The Beatles, A Hard Day's Night sounding tinny and flat. I move quickly forward towards two closed doors. Reaching the first, I press my ear against the numb, grey metal. The music pulls from beyond the door. Is this their cell? Is this my trap? Has my path inside been too easy? I grab the handle, force it down then barge the door open. Inside lies the cheapest of cargo, men!

A bare room, a store room, fifteen by ten. Twenty black men are chained and shackled together. Not in irons but in shiny new steel. All sit listless and mute on the floor. Dirty, white canvas sacks mask their faces. Each one dressed in cheap blue jeans, a plain black t-shirt and new, white, brandless trainers. My entrance causes only a hushed, ripple of movement. The room is heated and warm. The music piped in from a single wall-mounted speaker, which faces a single CCTV camera.

And now, what now? Escape with men and disease? Free what? Save who? No one here! No one at all! Twenty-one bullets - twenty and me. Footsteps pound against metal - the tide rushing in. Twenty-one bullets to fight my way out or twenty-one bullets to stop the disease.

I move to pull a sack off the nearest man but stop, with the thought the eyes, too human the stare, I stop. I pull the second gun. I use it first. Without a silencer, the screams are mauled by the bang. One to the head, another to the head, one to the head, another to the head. Panic. The instinct to flee and protest. The listless and the mute, the gagged and the shackled. No voice to plea, no room for flight. The heated room no good for meat. The soiled white sacks shatter and burst. Brains explode the soul. One by one I commit to death.

All done, job done. But me? Twenty-one for twenty and me? The tide reaches the shore. The door opens sharply and spits in a grenade. Decision made; I have no will or movement, no flight or fight, just the blank sense of emptying.

CHAPTER TWENTY-ONE

In darkness, I sit. A blindfold pins black into my eyes. Lashings of heavy, wet rope bond my arms and legs to a chair. Struggle is futile. Cold water soaks a shiver deep into my bones. I sense movement behind me. The black is ripped from my eyes. I see the room, the same as before, although the air has been chilled to keep us fresh. Sitting opposite me, I see a man, a Savile Row gent, of sixty plus untroubled years. He sits with an eerie calm, completely relaxed and at ease. No anger or aggression debases his demeanor; no carpet of death ruffles his poise.

'Well, well,' he speaks. 'So, this is you, Samuel Dean. What are we to make of you, Mr. Dean? What are we to make of you?'

He speaks with an English accent, well-spoken but not so posh as to grate. He continues,

'My name, and it's my real name, is Fox, Mr. Fox….I tell you that out of respect. You see, as a well-travelled, old cynic people rarely surprise me. Indeed, I find most to be flat and predictable, but you, not you. No. You, Mr. Dean, you stepped far beyond the role I assigned you. Of course, I can't be too gracious, you did after all cause us problems, damage, too, so naturally we must reciprocate somewhat, but still, well done, and thank you.'

He smiles warmly like we could be friends.

'We made you an offer, which you rejected, be appeased or be killed. It was a good, honest offer, but still, you chose to pursue your innocence. A decision, which I have to say, somewhat tarnishes the respect I have for you, innocence is, after all, highly overrated. In fact, I would say, it is meaningless, as is guilt. It's good, of course, that you had the will to fight, to kill for something that you thought was important, but innocence, when so much more could have been yours. Strange, well, quaint. Me, personally, I have no respect for innocence or guilt. None at all. Desire and need, Mr. Dean. Desire and need, that is what I respect, that is what I recognize. And what is it we need? We need to survive. And what is it we desire? Well, so many things! But then, to be a man, Mr. Dean, to be a man.

You, you are a poor man. Your financials stink, as does your education. Use them to assess your position in the world, as people would, and the only conclusion one can honestly draw is that you dwell at the base the food chain, that you must be physically or mentally infirm, a social or mental retard, one of life's lost and defeated drones. But actually, I myself, I would put you in the top five or six percent, after all, who would succeed in hunting you? Us, well yes, of course, but still, what a waste you potentially are. Hitler, he once observed that communists, once corrected, made the most excellent Nazis. He could have just shot them of course, but then a useful resource is always worth investing in so with that in mind, let me offer you an explanation. We, what you hunt, we are the future. We are the wealth, the intellect; we are the force. We are the collective who will ensure a future exists for us, for humanity. Put simply, people, too many people, too many irrelevant,

unproductive, all-consuming people. We may share a world, but that world is not enough. There are too many people. Soon, we know, nature will snap, and that snap, that recoil will cause untold damage and misery. Chaos will ferment, and war will offer the only solution. Another war to control our planet's precious recourses: water, minerals, the earth itself. What else do you expect our governments to do? How else do you expect them to appease the people? The earth cannot carry the weight of us all. But with our knowledge, with our technology, think how well we could live if we were so many fewer. A Malthusian Check is coming, this is certain, and from it, we may see the final destruction of us all, of all humanity. Our only hope, Mr. Dean, is to control the adjustment, to manage the cull, to remove billions from the equation. And soon, we will be ready. Against us stands what? You? You may have scored a small success but still, we breathe, Mr. Dean, and we prosper. We are winning the debate where the debate needs to be won. So let me assure you, the few, we will stand as giants.'

We lock stares. I offer no deceit. I hide no hate.

'I could hurt you in so many ways. I could take your DNA, I could splice it into a cell and eventually, nine months later, I could watch as your child is born. Whether I choose to let your child live or die is not a matter for us now, but still, how far do you think I would go? Beyond the grave?...Presence of mind, of purpose. Take the Spartans, if a baby was born who was obviously below par, their standard being based on a warrior ethic, then they would throw the baby off a cliff. So simple, and direct, honest, for the good of the people. While we, we do so over complicate matters, don't you think? There was a video on the phone of Mr. Brockhurst, which I believe you watched. Strange man Henry, he found God straight out of thin air. He wasn't at the bottom of the pit, he wasn't a loser, a loner, a drunk or an addict, not like your usual born again convert. No, he was successful, sharp, completely focused, but then from nowhere he found God, or as he put it, God found him. Strange. Another surprise. I soon expect a third. Anyway, the video, guess what, it's going to happen. A small test. It won't give us our billions, not alone, but still, tens of thousands that's hardly a bad day at the office...Of course, you shouldn't think we enjoy what we do. We don't. It doesn't serve our ego, not like

Oakley, he got carried away with the self, with living the dream of power. Us, what we do, we do for the good of humanity, not for the good of ourselves, something I am sure you can understand.

He passes a casual stare over the men killed by me.

'You caused us problems and damage, and now we must reciprocate. Your inability to talk makes you the perfect dummy, the perfect practice doll. But let me tell you this, if you survive, and further prove your spirit, I may just offer you a view, a chance to see the reality of our power, indeed the beauty of our power and the inevitability of our victory. I will then ask you a question, Mr. Dean, will you be appeased or will you be killed?'

Behind me movement pounces. Before I can turn and look, a blindfold grabs and smothers my eyes.

CHAPTER TWENTY-TWO

I know what this is, torture. Pain. Good. Justice. A beautiful scream. Does the mute scream? Beyond words to the base of man. A scream to wring out sin. I have nothing to say, never, to anyone! I give them no sound, nothing of me. My blood, spit and sweat but nothing of me. You survive, or you don't. All I think is that I would do it to them.

Darkness. Baking hot in a metal tomb. My guess, a shipping container. Definitely out at sea. Drifting in and out of black. Hungry, thirsty, but better than before, now always better than before. Alone, just me. They give me time.

CHAPTER TWENTY-THREE

A slow fade back into life. The air is free and plentiful. A warm breeze moistens my eyes and stings my parched, cracked skin. Trimmed, lush green grass offers my aching body a slither of comfort. I am felled, slumped in the fetal position. The warm earth soothes my grateful limbs. My sight stutters clumsily to realize the view: a green, blue, earthly vision. No need for heaven when this close to Earth. From high on a hill, I look down on a rush of nature, on trees, grass, bush and plant. Every hue is ripe with life. Then buildings - a town, like a pixelated image, white, grey and brown dots scattered, unplanned. People, the chaos of people. Good for people. Shelter, from the other side of nature. And then a sea, finally a blue, sparkling sea touches the sky and closes the horizon. Is this Africa? Have they brought me? Why?

My feet are chained to the earth. My cell is a ruin. Three stone walls, one behind and two others on either side, enclose me. On a small, folding picnic table is laid out a laptop, binoculars, a picnic hamper, a bottle of water and a bottle of champagne, both chilling in a bucket of ice.

A helicopter tears through the sky. I look up and catch a flash of military green, this leaden, dead weight forced through space.

Without thinking, I crawl to the table and snatch the bottle of water. It is mine to consume, and I do so in one. It almost hurts, to feel it thawing this dead in my flesh.

Although irregular in height, the three walls all stand at least seven foot tall. In one, I see a small window, made to look toothless by a single rusty iron bar. I take to my feet, like the new born beast, unsure and unsteady, but still feral. No pain has the force to kick me down, so I jump up and take a hold of the wall, my arms hooked through the window. Scanning the view beyond, I see the ruin continue. Could it once have been a colonial fort? In the near distance, I see a group of twenty or so men, middle-aged to old, both white, black and Asian. They sit at tables enjoying food and champagne. All face towards the sea, all hold or wear binoculars. They could be a group of bankers snorting up a day at the races. One of them looks like Spitz, but no sign of Fox. Surrounding them are a dozen or so heavily armed men, both Black and White. The black men wear green military uniforms, the whites a mix of jeans, casual shirts and stone coloured bush clothes. Behind them, three civilian helicopters wait still on the ground.

As I let myself fall, I grab the iron bar and yank it from its root. Although partly decaying with rust it still has weight and, being sharp at one end, could prove a useful tool. Hearing footsteps and chatter, I drop it to the ground and kick it to the base of a wall.

Into the fourth empty wall steps Fox - dressed impeccably in a beige linen suit and holding a glass of what, I guess, is champagne. He flashes a happy smile, one lubricated with drink. He could be at the wedding of a well-loved niece. Behind him, stands one of the guards, a white man, who aims at me a rifle and a stare that seethes with hate. Fox speaks to me:

'Ah, Mr. Dean. You wake, alive! Well done. Congratulations! In time to witness a bright, new day. A new dawn, Mr. Dean, set to rise from the horizon in exactly,' he looks at his watch, then adds, 'fifty eight minutes time…Don't worry, you are perfectly safe. I can assure you we have everything under control. So relax, replenish yourself. Savour the moment. Hear our call to history!'

He smiles, knowingly then takes a sip of champagne.

'Today, people will die, as they do every day, every single day, but you, you, I know, will have the strength to see beyond the death, to see beyond the devastation. You, Mr. Dean, will have the strength of mind to witness the truth, to see an act of kindness, one from humanity, to humanity, from the present, to the future…..A minor blip anyway, because in time, when our mission is concluded, a seam of human sacrifice will plate the entire earth…A seam that it will be stronger than any rock, more valuable than any fuel, and on which, Mr. Dean, we will lay the foundations for a secure and prosperous future. So, to us, Mr. Dean, to us!'

He raises his glass aloft. I remain passive, neither accepting nor rejecting his words.

'The laptop will show you the island fall and then, the tsunami, it is yours to witness live. The greatest show on earth, Mr. Dean. Who needs that Jackson fellow now.'

He laughs, highly amused at himself. He then turns and ambles away. The guard watches him go but keeps the rifle leering at me.

The chain that binds me to the cell is about three metres in length and bolted firmly to the back wall. Fully extended my reach would just about breach the fourth, empty wall. Not enough, this time, to grab the guard who now turns to me, reaches in to his shirt breast pocket, pulls out a set of two keys and throws them towards me. I catch them without effort. He speaks, with a South African accent.

'Yours. Go. Free yourself. I'll give you ten, fifteen minutes, I promise. Then, it's you and me.'

He wants me dead. Even so, I'm tempted. But still, I'll need more than what is currently offered, so I toss the keys back. I must let him think, I am now appeased. I throw the keys to fall just short of his reach. He takes the bait, lunges forward to catch them, but misses. How easy it is to bruise a man. After snatching the keys from the ground, he looks at me and speaks.

'Good men are dead because of you. You will never be one of us!'

He turns his back to face me then steps slowly away putting the keys back into his shirt breast pocket.

I move to the iron bar, sit and retrieve it. The guard stands ten metres from the cell, casting his stare towards the horizon. The bar could be fashioned into a knife, well a crude stabbing weapon, but nothing that would extend my reach. I look around. Could a champagne cork carry a blade? A short distance maybe, but with accuracy and force?

I twist and snap off a rusty piece of the bar, a three inch blade that will work as an arrowhead. As I sharpen the tip against the stone wall, the guard suddenly turns and looks at me. I stop and match his stare. His suspicion turns to contempt, and he looks away, back towards the sea.

I grab the bottle of champagne, strip away the foil then carefully remove the wire. Pushing the blade into the cork is tricky and takes considerable force, but finally it stands embedded, an inch deep. With my thumb held against the cork, I shake the bottle to give rage to the fizz.

Now to laugh, to force a laugh. I stand and walk as far as the chain will allow me, nose-to-nose with the fourth empty wall. I have my stage, my audience of one. This should be easy, I know the ante. Laugh for the people, for the silent people. Bruise this man and reel him in. But silence, still silence. Even held against this insanity, silence, still silence. No laugh or cry. He snaps his head around and looks at me, scowling like an animal chained and unable to attack. I fake a smile, a broad easy smile. I shake the champagne, full of cold, empty celebration. Then something ridiculous, a memory flashes - just me and my mother free and laughing. She told a joke, 'why was the baby strawberry crying? Because his mother was in a jam.' It comes, a stupid laugh. A man laughing to himself in a crowded room, crazed and uncensored. Thank you, mother, and on your behalf fuck them, fuck them all. Hear me laugh. Hear me mock you!

Confusion glazes the guard's face. Then, as is typical with such a man, the confusion fires anger and propels him towards me. Laughing, I continue to shake the bottle, the arrowhead concealed behind a palm, the cork desperate to burst but held against my thumb. With the gap between as nearly dead, he swings the rifle around so that the butt is ready to beat me. With the attack a step away, I release the cork, aimed towards his face. His instinct is sharp, his reaction swift. Sensing my plan, he twists his upper body away. His face is saved, but the back of his head takes the rusty blade. A painful grunt bellows from deep within his body as instinct rushes a hand towards the wound. I grab the hand and pull him towards me. The arrowhead hangs from the back of his head, less than an inch into his skull. Twisting to face me, he thrusts the rifle towards my head. Using the bottle,

I block the blow. The top half shatters; I ram what remains deep into his face. Pulling him close, I use my free hand to gag his rage. Attempting to throw him to the ground, I fail. I can barely contain his struggle. With the cork close to my mouth, I clamp it between my teeth then push my head forward stabbing the blade fully into his skull. His body is shocked into a seizure. It shakes violently, both alive and as dead as Frankenstein's monster.

With the keys now mine, I free myself from the chain, grab the binoculars then return to the body to scavenge all weapons. In a holster belt, I find an automatic handgun, extra ammunition and a large hunting knife. I strip it from the body and strap it to my waist. The rifle I carry in my hands.

From the cell, I flee; I run away. Down the hill and towards the coast. My plan, unknown. A dirt track provides a clear, rugged path. Dense forest on either side offers cover if needed. My pace is quick and steady. Heavy tyre tracks provide a smooth running surface. I look at my watch; I have fifty minutes left.

I have no mind to feel pain or to yield to fatigue. My mind is clear, tuned and set to detect any hint of pursuit. I am enclosed in an ever changing room, a tunnel of twisting track, arcing forest and a line of bright, white sky that hangs above me like an endless fluorescent tube.

The track levels out, and I leave the hill behind. The forest thins and merges into grassland. Turning to look behind, I doubt their need to pursue me. What threat can I be? How can I stop these men now teamed with nature? I have no answers only to run harder and faster. I have forty-three minutes left.

A dozen head of grazing cattle pauses to watch me pass. From behind them, appear a group of six carefree kids, as sunny as the day and shabbily dressed in Western hand-me-downs. Two carry long, thin sticks. Seeing me they catch a breeze and playfully give chase. I accelerate and leave them behind.

The town is built on the tip of a small peninsula. To avoid its streets, and to reach the coastline as quickly as I can, I veer from the path and continue across the rough contours of the open country. Again I trespass, into the green of pasture, waist-high grasses, bushes and trees. A pitch for players to hide, hunt and feed. What lays hidden, poised beneath the grass? Nothing as wild as that playing on the hill.

A small incline elevates my view. I pause and aim the binoculars towards the coast. In a small, natural bay a seaplane floats on a calm, blue sea. A black wooden jetty acts as a bridge to the land. A white man, carefully preened in jeans, white t-shirt and aviator shades, stands on one of the plane's landing floats. He crouches down and examines what looks to be a video camera fixed to the plane's undercarriage. Is this their means to film the island fall? A twin-engine, fixed-wing plane that could carry, I guess, the pilot plus eight to ten others. The windows, which are car-like, a windscreen plus two on either side are blackened so give nothing away. The man stands up straight, reaches into his waistband and pulls out a handgun. With it, he gestures to those inside to move on out. A side door is pushed open. The man climbs on-board, pulling the door shut. The propeller flashes into life, speeding into a blur. I have four hundred metres to race. I go, running. The land with its contours, trees and grass gives me a chance to approach unseen.

I take the first hundred, and the plane stays still. I take the second hundred, and the plane stays still. Why, for safety checks or to draw me in? I take the third hundred, and the plane begins to turn. The line-of-sight moves in my favour. Distance, I fear, does not. I demand more speed, but nothing comes. The land then delivers a smooth, gentle slope that files me towards the line.

I reach the jetty. The engine revs higher. I hesitate, and now, what now? Shoot my way in? The plane begins to taxi. I have no choice; I discard the rifle then lunge towards the plane. Hitting the water, my hand hooks me to a strut which connects the undercarriage to a float. The plane accelerates sharply away. Water piles over my body, nearly breaking my grip. I manage to hook another hand then haul myself up on to the float. Water screams at me time to get off. I barely resist. Finally, the force of water is replaced by the weaker rush of the air.

Looking down, the land seems smaller and yet more massive. The town is just one of several spilling over the land. I see people, their faces playing in my mind. Not one is an ant or insect to crush. If I must kill, and why, I must, then I must kill the gods and save the people.

Looking forward, I see the island, a cone-like structure with a flattened tip. Although small in the distance, I feel its size - a billion tones formed over a million years. I check my watch, I have thirty-five minutes left. Reaching the Island, this mountain of the sea, consumes another ten.

Needing the plane to land, I loosen my grip then carefully inch my body, feet first, through the now thick, angry air. Reaching the camera, I release a kick which continues until the camera hangs limply from its fixing. A minute passes before the plane begins to descend.

From the holster, I pull the handgun. Knowing it was submerged in water, I pull the trigger to test it works. It does, and a bullet flies wasted into nothing.

Fearful the landing will rip me from the plane and further wet the gun, I decide to use the gun while I can. With the plane just twenty metres from the sea, I take aim and fire. Bullets rip through the undercarriage, up into the plane where the passengers sit. Their reaction is swift, bullets roar back. One slashes my right thigh nearly knocking me from the float. Hooked by a single, slipping hand I manage to pound the remaining bullets into the plane, saving the final flurry for the pilot. I then fall ten metres and crash the sea.

I feel still, cocooned in cool, sinuous water. Reaching the bottom of my fall, I pause for a brief, calm moment before a sharp, burning pain jolts my body to kick and grab for the surface.

Breaking into the air, I see the plane land rough and hard, gorging a furrow deep into the sea. Suddenly, it spins rotating on its axis. I push the gun into the holster then set off in pursuit, swimming towards the plane and island.

As I reach the shallows, the plane slows to a halt. I take to my feet, barging my way through water stained red by the blood seeping from my thigh.

Now running, I pull the gun from the holster and load a fresh magazine. With the plane only metres a way I hear a man scream, pleading:

'No!! Don't!! I can fly us!!'

To test the gun, I pull the trigger. It jams. I grab the knife and reach the plane. The pleading man, pleads some more:

'No!! Please!! I can fly us!!'

Stepping onto a float, I lunge for a side door, grab the handle and, with gun pointing, pull the door open. Inside, a handgun waits raised and aimed at my face. It is held by the preened white man. He sits on the back seat; his clothes are covered in blood. His eyes stare maddened, forced wide open to catch the final light, the closing moments of life. Between us is another man, a dead lump, ahead of us in the darkness. The white man speaks, punching his words towards me:

'So, this is the cunt!'

On the front seat a nerdy looking man, no soldier, watches us with panic and fear. Next to him, the pilot lies dead.

We pause, our guns aimed and waiting for a command. In his other hand, the white man holds what looks like a handheld radio. Glancing at my gun, he speaks.

'Does it work?'

A spiteful shriek of laughter briefly covers his pain. He then speaks again.

'There's nothing you can do! You can't stop it. No one can stop it. But me, I can start it.'

The other man replies, again pleading.

'I can fly the plane! I can get us out of here!'

'Then fuck off!'

This other man turns to me.

'I'm not one of them. They made me do it!'

The white man replies.

'Made him. Paid him! A fuckin' geologist! He could help but fuck him! You're all comin' with me!'

He releases the radio letting it rest on his lap. A radio? No. A device to fire the explosives and blow the island: a digital clock counting down to zero, a keypad, an antenna, a large red button protected by a plastic cover and a metal key. He grabs the key and turns it.

The geologist screams a final demand.

'No!'

Then brings a third handgun into the fray, nervously aimed at the white man who responds with hateful contempt.

'Two guns that won't work.'

Even so, he pauses, weighing up the odds. Fear, he calls, wins. He flips the plastic cover and exposes the red button. Bang! A bullet puts pay to the light. The geologist freezes, distraught at having to kill so close to death. But how quickly we learn and soon the gun is tracking towards me. I make my move slashing the knife towards his face. I win, cutting his throat. He drops the gun and grabs the wound, a fool trying to catch and save his blood. I snap the plastic cover back over the button. The countdown shows I have twenty-three minutes left. The geologist shakes with pathological shock. His wound is gruesome but not, I suspect, fatal.

I search for and find a first aid kit. From it, I take two bandages. The first I use on the geologist, who is now a mute, submissive wreck, the second I use to plug the hole in my thigh.

And now, what now? Grab all the guns I can, three handguns and nine magazines. The emptied first aid kit acts as a case. Finally, I hook the detonator to my belt, pull the key from the plane's ignition then leave the geologist to live or die.

The island seems vast and inhuman. But once, eternal and beyond the power of man.

What can I do? First what do I know? When using explosives to demolish a building or a rock face a series of relatively small explosions, timed to explode in an exact and precise sequence is used. This, if used here, could give me a chance. If I can interrupt or break the sequence then maybe the island will hold.

I head for the summit, a good hundred and fifty metres high, over steep, grey, barren rock that is slippery underfoot and has little to offer a hand. As I go, I scan the ground looking for drill holes, for surely the explosives must be planted deep beneath the surface.

With fifty metres complete, I pause to catch my breath. I check the clock, I have nineteen minutes left.

As I continue to climb, I feel increasingly exposed, at odds with the vastness that surrounds me. Like the child, dizzy at the thought of infinity. All that contains me seems still and at ease, silent, suffocating.

As I near the summit, the incline flattens, so an easier place to drill. With the tsunami aimed at the mainland, the side of the island primed ready to fall must also face the people.

I fall to my knees to examine my find, a brown plastic disc fixed to the ground by a single screw. I grab the disc and rip it free. Beneath it is a hole, eight inches wide and drilled deep into the ground. A length of nylon rope bolted to the top of the hole extends down into the darkness. I grab it and pull. It carries weight, fifteen kilos minimum. As I haul the weight to the surface, I count each pull, taking each as a metre. Thirty pulls later and a copper cylinder, six inches in diameter and half a metre in length reaches the light. I pause, holding a bomb.

Extending through the top of the cylinder is a thin metal tube on which is fixed a small collection of electronic components. Is this the detonator and the electronics to control it? Seeing that the top of the cylinder is lipped, I twist it to see if it gives, it does, so I slowly continue to unscrew it. The thin metal tube remains still as the top rotates around it. Once free, I slowly lift the top away. Inside, I see the explosive, a compacted, white crystalline material into which the thin metal tube is pressed. With a gentle grip, I take hold of the tube. Fear then forces hesitation. Could a spark explode the fuel? Suddenly, ahead of my thoughts, I yank the tube free of the bomb.

One beat in the sequence is dead.

Leaving the detonator and cylinder apart on the ground, I take to my feet and sprint in search of the next hole. Ten metres along, I find it. Without stopping, I continue ahead. Another ten metres and another hole, and so on and so on and so on. If this pattern continues, then some fifty holes must cradle a bomb. I check the clock; I have fifteen minutes left.

Pulling a gun from the case, I move to the nearest hole. I rip the plastic cover free then fire a single shot into the darkness and towards the bomb. Nothing. No sound, no explosion, nothing. Another bullet but again, nothing. In frustration, I pull the trigger until the gun clicks empty but still, the bomb remains live.

In the sky, near the mainland an object catches my eye. A helicopter is racing towards me.

Grabbing the rope, I haul the cylinder to the surface - forty pulls, stealing a minute. As soon as the detonator comes into view, I snatch it from the bomb and discard it, jabbing it hard into the air. Leaving the cylinder on the ground, I get ready, go! Exploding from the blocks like a sprinter to the sound of a starter gun - an actual bang. Twisting my head to locate the sound, I see a fading cloud of grey smoke rising above the detonator. Is this the spark, the switch to destruction? Of course. A small, volatile explosive used to snap a more stable mass.

No bullet, not mine, would strike such a thin metal tube, but a rock?

From the ground, I choose my weapon, a rock just small enough to fit the hole and a good eight kilos in weight.

Smashing the plastic cover with my foot, I then drop and release the rock. Three seconds later the ground shudders and quakes. A flume of grey smoke and shattered rock flees the hole. A second beat in the sequence is dead.

I sprint twenty metres to another hole. Only smaller, lighter rocks lay near-by. I take the largest, tear off the plastic cover then send the rock falling. As soon as it leaves my grip I go, sprinting to take the next twenty metres. Beneath me the ground vibrates. Another beat in the sequence is dead.

I continue, on and on, the fog of desire numbing my pain; the fear of death mauled by a raging need for victory.

As I drop the rock to snap the eighth beat dead, the helicopter looms ever near, a military green predator effortlessly rushing to strike.

With time edging ahead of me, and the sequence still long and intact, I decide to extend my run, to leave two in the sequence live.

I continue on and on, lost in the fog. Come, time, come. I am touched only by the present.

Fourteen beats now dead. Working the fifteenth, the bullets come, a poorly aimed volley from an ever nearing machinegun. With the rock falling, I take off. Bullets track my path.

Completing the thirty metres, I dive towards the next hole. Bullets shatter rock beneath me. Close but not close enough. I destroy the beat then sprint away.

I look at the clock; I have ninety seconds left.

The bullets pause, waiting for me, the soon-to-be point blank dummy. Reaching the hole, I destroy the bomb then rise and sprint away.

Have I done enough? Can I take one more? The helicopter slows to a hover, thirty metres above me, the sword of Damocles waiting to fall.

Another hole. I hit the ground, my body collapsing. I pull the cover free then look for a rock. Finding one, I leave it; instead I grab the rope and haul the bomb up towards the light. The helicopter hangs still in the air, poised to savour the kill. It begins to turn, to bring the gunman into view, to hand him an easy shot.

As I face my executioner, the bomb reaches the surface. I wrap my hands around the cold copper casing then, ripping all energy from me, launch it high into the air. As it rises towards the helicopter, I move a hand to the detonator, flick the cover then press the switch. And now, what now, have I done enough?

I cower to the ground, arms covering my head. The explosives fire. A shockwave from above flattens me, grinding me into the rock, from which a dense, physical sound is flushed. I look up at the sky; the helicopter is twisted in the air and plunging towards me. I race to my feet then burst away. Flumes of smoke and broken rock line the run of holes. Reaching the summit, I dive over the edge. Behind me, the helicopter smashes into the ground. I plunge several metres before the filled in crater violently halts my fall.

Has it held? I stare at the ground, at the grey, blank rock, my mind concussed, my body shattered and gasping for air. I cannot look or see. The ground is still. The loudest noise is the helicopter crumbling towards the sea. I wait, for some time I wait, then twist on to my back and look up at the sky. Smoke and dust cloud the air but the ground, the earth is still and solid. The island has held. It has stood against man. A thought then suddenly appears, I have saved enough to kill some more. I must, and can, kill some more.

I stand, rising through the pain that my body screams. Limping away, I see a stash of unused copper cylinders piled on the ground. As I near them, I see that each has a detonator. Are they bombs? They are. I remove a detonator, throw it hard into rock and watch it explode. With three such bombs tightly gripped, I stagger away, back towards the plane.

With a lack of care, but no diminished need to kill once more, I shuffle and slide down towards the sea.

As I near the plane, I pass the bodies of its crew, now lumbering in the shallows. The side passenger door is pushed respectfully open. So what, is this what it takes to get staff?

I load the bombs into the plane; the Geologist watches me, fearful and compliant. I pull the ignition key from my pocket and hold it towards him. He hesitates for a second, but then takes it, gladly. He knows his job and doesn't complain. Once airborne, he takes my directions, and we fly towards the mountain.

Should I fall with the bombs? Guide them to a final destination? Who, in me, is left? Only my innocence, my proof that I didn't kill, her the Woman. That is my rebooting. That may allow me to live with the noise.

The fools, they remain, waiting and watching. They've paid their money and now demand a show.

We pass high overhead. Then turn to retrace our path. As we approach, I direct the geologist to fly low and fast. We are open and obvious and quickly seen. I expect gunfire to rage our way, but instead they stand and stare, confused and bewildered. Using a handgun, I shoot the glass from a side window. Finally, a rogue mercenary pumps bullets our way. Thirty metres from the ground and fifty to reach the crowd below, I release the bombs. Man and earth are churned and scattered.

The geologist looks at me with a nod of his head, as if right has been done, as if we are now a team. I blank him.

And now, what now? End it, fly me back to Malta.

CHAPTER TWENTY-FOUR

Fifteen hours, drone-like. Inside a drone. I am a drone. This constant hum is mine. No gratitude for the plane, set-up to take them back to Malta, all the way, non-stop, now hijacked by me. No thanks at all. Water, food and sleep can't calm the anger I have for land. I want my hands digging the earth, to touch, and feel, my innocence. I need to see the proof. I need to return to me.

The geologist conforms. Does nothing to make my trigger-happy hand twitch or snap. But still, I consider his fate. Should I kill him? Should he be my final kill? The very last one. He's done enough, now how shall he pay?

CHAPTER TWENTY-FIVE

We land, half a mile from shore. The breaking dawn gives us just enough light. We could taxi to land, but instead, I take to the sea and leave it all behind: the plane, the guns, the Geologist. I am free, as is he, free to explain, free to know my truth.

The swim is a race, between me and me. Needless, but me, as fast as I can go. I am victorious; land is my prize - back on the quayside where I once did kill.

The stone steps, embedded in time, return me to the tourist perch, which is deserted and perfect, just me alone. An audience will come soon enough, a crowd to cross-out the wrongs scarring my name.

Out at sea, the dawn light lifts the plane into my sight. It rides a still tide to nowhere. All is peaceful and calm, but inside, can he live with himself? If so, can he speak for me? Not that I need him; not that I need anyone.

At the flowerbed, I take to my knees. The earth is cool and moist. I dig down, down into the earth. Digging down, deeper than before? Definitely deeper than before. Too deep now. Now a metal box. I pull it up. A plain, metal box, heavy with something inside. I rip the lid free and see a gun, a phone, ammunition, a credit card, a passport with my photo and the name James Jones. The phone rings. I see the number on the screen, the same as the one given to me by the Sailor Man. I answer. He speaks:

'Sam, I know it's you. I can see you.'

I could look around, but why? Why?!

'It's me, you know who, your friend. I helped you. I gave you the gun. I provided you transport, the boat and the cars.'

I know who this is, now why?!

'When I say me, of course, I mean us. It was us who helped you. We, the people who share your enemy, who you fought. The other side. The counter force. If you like, the good.'

The good? Am I the good? Prove it!

'You found a war, a secret war. You were an innocent, pulled in, and yet you scored a significant victory. However, the victory is far from complete. The war continues, we still must fight. But you, what now for you? The police, the authorities, some function of government? That can never be. We can never allow that, Sam. This is not about governments; it is so much bigger than that. The war continues, and we need you. We all need you, Sam. This phone contains a list of names and addresses. We took them from Oakley's website. You gave them to us, Sam. We were watching. We had high hopes for you, and you didn't let us down. The people on the list, they are all the enemy. Each and every one acts against humanity, as they, those you killed, acted against humanity. We will give you everything you need to eliminate them. Your name, Samuel Dean, Samuel Dean is dead. The evidence you left has been destroyed. I repeat, destroyed. We had no other option. We couldn't let you lose. The evidence would never have given you what you wanted. That man is now dead, but you, you live to do good. We now offer you a role. We offer you a purpose. You have everything you need for the first name on the list, to eliminate him...We can end this, James, we can end it, and we will, together, we will complete the victory.'

He ends the call. I look at the phone, is it hacked? The screen navigates to show the list, scores of names and addresses. I hear a noise, I think I do. I grab the gun and turn. Nothing. I see nothing. Out at sea, the plane has gone, it has vanished.

THE END

Printed in Great Britain
by Amazon